With This Ring, I Thee Wed

By

Linda Salinas

Copyright © 2019 Linda Salinas

ISBN-13: 9781796973709

In Memory Of

My Brother Randell Johnson

July 23, 1950-April 30, 2014

Acknowledgments

I want to thank my friends who read my first book and gave me their critique: Linda Adkins, Cathy Bryce, Julie Burton, Gena Gardiner, Gloria McNutt, Mary Richey, Carrie Durley, and Marilyn Brannigan.

I want to thank Mary's husband, Mike, who texted me at 6:30 one morning to tell me that Mary woke up at 5:00am to finish reading the book, but she was bawling---not just crying. Every time he looked at her, she would cry more. He didn't want to leave her alone, and he needed to get to his job, so he asked if I could please call her on the phone to talk to her. I called her, and we laughed for at least thirty minutes---mainly about the reaction her husband had to her crying. Then we discussed what she liked best about the book. That was the first book: The Diary in the Old Valentine Box. Her reaction gave me the initiative to finish the second book and now this is the third.

I want to thank my husband, Albert, who puts up with me and my incessant typing; my daughter, Carla, who is a writer herself; and my sister, Brenda, who gave me encouragement.

And finally, thanks to my mother for being my mother.

With this Ring, I Thee Wed

Chapter 1
First Day

Excitement is in the air. Summer vacation has come to an end and thousands of students are converging on the university campus. Many of them are freshman and have mixed emotions of nervousness, excitement, anxiety, and also a little fear! They just don't know what to expect. Most of the young freshmen are away from home and away from parents for the first time. They don't have the convenience of having their own bedroom and own private bathroom, like many of them had at home with their parents. Now, they are sharing a *small* room with a perfect stranger in some instances, and then they are sharing a community bathroom at the end of the hall. What a change! What a growing experience!

Marilyn and her parents participated in a campus visit when trying to choose the right university for her, but nothing compared to the feeling she had when she actually started moving her things into her dorm room. At least she had talked to her new roommate and they got to know each other over the phone. Luckily, they had many things in common—loved horses, loved pets, loved art, and wanted to become high school teachers. They even coordinated their bedspreads, so their dorm room looked 'put together.'

Marilyn was such an attractive young woman. Her blonde hair curved to the bottom of her cheek and wispy bangs fell gently over her eyebrows. Her beautiful blue eyes sparkled when she smiled. Her beautiful appearance was only a hint of her beautiful personality; she was a very kind and amiable person, always wanting to help others. In high school, the required one-hundred hours of community service stretched to over three-hundred hours for Marilyn. She enjoyed community service.

Marilyn was unpacking her suitcase and putting her clothes into her chest of drawers when her roommate entered the room.

"Debbie! You're here! I was sure hoping you'd show up!" Marilyn ran over to her and gave her a great big hug.

"Marilyn, I'm *soooo* excited to meet you in person. This is going to be a really great year! We are going to have so much fun!" Debbie answered enthusiastically. Both girls giggled as they put their clothes in their miniature closets---quite different from their closets at home.

"Minimalistic!" Marilyn said. "Keep that word in your mind!" They laughed. It was obvious that these two girls were going to be perfect for each other.

After they put their clothes away, and all of the other stuff that they brought, they decided to walk through the campus. So off they went! They were so excited. The campus was so huge! Everywhere they looked, they saw hundreds of students laughing and screaming in some instances. Kids were unloading their cars and dragging clothes over their shoulders to their dorms. Parents were helping move boxes and were chatting with other parents. Actually, the parents were just as excited. There was an element of electricity in the air. New semester! New students!

As Marilyn and Debbie walked along the pathways, they were amazed at the buildings, the statues, the trees, and walkways. They wondered what buildings they would have classes in and if they would have any classes together. They would know the next day when they picked up their schedules. Surely, they would have some classes together!

After roaming around the campus, the girls found their way back to the dormitory and crashed on their beds. "Whew!" Marilyn said. "I bet I lose weight this year. I think we will be doing a lot of walking around here. You know that freshman fifteen they talk about? I don't think it is going to happen to us!"

"You mean the fifteen pounds that they say freshman gain during the year because they eat so much?" Debbie asked.

9

"Exactly," Marilyn said.

"Speaking of eating," Debbie said kiddingly, "let's go get something to eat!"

Marilyn sprang up from the bed and said, "I'm game. Let's go!"

The girls grabbed their purses and headed out the door and down the hallway. They walked down the street to the nearest hamburger place. They walked in the door, found a booth near the back, and laughed as they talked about their day. Just when their food arrived at the table, a couple of really handsome guys came walking through the door.

"Marilyn, don't look obvious, but look at those two handsome guys walking through the door," Debbie said glancing away from the door.

Marilyn nonchalantly looked in the direction of the door. "Uh huh, I see what ya mean," she answered. "Can we manage to get in a class with those guys?"

"Where there is a will, there is a way," Debbie answered. "Haven't we heard that before?"

"OK, mark that down. Goal #1 is finding out what those guys are studying and what class they are going to be in," Marilyn demanded.

The girls finished their hamburger and decided to head back to the dorm. As they walked to the front to leave, they had to walk past the two guys. Marilyn couldn't help but notice how handsome the guys were---especially the tall one with the almost black hair. His eyes were a deep brown color. As Marilyn walked past him, their eyes met. She definitely felt a surge of electricity. *What just happened? Oh my gosh!*

"Cute, huh?" Debbie said.

The girls walked back to the dorm and changed into their pajamas. "It's jammy time!" Marilyn said. They were both tired and were anxious to jump into bed. Plus, they couldn't wait for the new day.

Chapter Two
Young Love

Sunshine streamed through the window and danced on the wall waking the girls early. They jumped up, dressed quickly to head out of the door, and almost ran down the hallway. They were more than anxious to find out their schedule of classes for their first semester. Walking into the auditorium, they quickly registered and then took their place in line to finalize their course selections.

"Looks like if this schedule goes through, we will have at least two classes together. That's great!" Debbie exclaimed. "Now we can study together, too."

Just as the girls made it up to the head table, Debbie noticed the same two guys that they had seen the night before standing in the line next to them. "Don't look now, Marilyn, but those two good-looking guys are standing in the line next to us."

The "*Don't look now, Marilyn,*" went right out the window. Marilyn immediately looked around and there they were----both looking directly at her. *Oh my gosh---there they are---he's looking right at me-ok---just smile,* Marilyn said to herself. She smiled and then looked away, because she was embarrassed. She hoped her face wasn't red because sometimes when she is embarrassed, her face gets red. *I hope I didn't look stupid. Did I look stupid?*

The girls got their schedules and headed out the door. The boys watched their every move.

Michael was tall, dark and very handsome. His almost jet-black hair was thick and was cut perfectly—not too short and not too long. His dark brown eyes were piercing. He remembered how he felt when his eyes met Marilyn's the night before. He felt that spark of electricity also; it was quite different from anything he had ever felt before.

"She is really beautiful, isn't she? Her friend is beautiful, too," Michael's friend Christopher said sincerely. Christopher was very attractive also, and his long, wavy blonde hair hung past his ears. His blue eyes were mesmerizing.

"Christopher, we really need to find out who those girls are," Michael said with conviction. "Let's find out what classes they're gonna be in."

"Are ya gonna enroll in her class?" Chris asked.

"Of course not, but I might just happen to be walking by the class when it's over or before it begins," Michael said. "Sounds like a good plan, doesn't it?" Christopher nodded his head in agreement. "Hey---I just remembered that I know someone in the registrar's office. He's a good friend of mine. I bet he can pull up her schedule, but first I have to find out what her name is."

Chapter Three
Coincidental Meeting

The first day of the school semester was just two days away. The girls studied their class schedules and mapped out where their classes were to be held. The campus map helped them find the shortest distance to each building. They would be walking most of the time but sometimes they could catch the campus bus to get to their classes on the other side of the campus. Either way, they'd have to hustle to make it on time.

They discussed their classes and made a note of the books that needed to be purchased at the campus bookstore. They gathered the supplies----pens, pencils, spiral notebooks, calculators---they thought they needed for the new semester. They were ready!

"OK, Marilyn," Debbie said. "We have a couple of days of freedom before we have to hit the books. What do ya think about going back to that hamburger place again tonight?"

"I know why you're saying that," Marilyn responded. "You think we're gonna run into those guys again, right?"

"No! Of course not! I want to go because the hamburgers are sooooo good." Debbie responded.

"Yeah, sure," Marilyn said with a wide grin on her face. They both bent over laughing. Hugging each other, they headed out the door.

As they walked through the campus and down the street to the hamburger place, Marilyn hoped they would see the handsome men again. *Wouldn't it be nice to run into those guys?* Marilyn thought to herself. *I promise to not look so stupid this time.*

Marilyn got to the door first but opened it and allowed Debbie to walk through. "Thanks, Marilyn. You are *so* kind."

"Just trying to be nice to my roommate," Marilyn replied smiling brightly. They walked to the back of the restaurant and sat in the booth near the window. *Great place to sit,* Marilyn thought. *We can see if anyone we're interested in is gonna come in.* She barely had that thought when she saw the two boys walk through the door. She felt her pulse racing. *Get a grip. Be cool.*

Just as the guys sat down in the booth closer to the front door, the girls' food was ready. Since customers were called by name, the restaurant worker called out, "Marilyn." Michael heard the name and then saw Marilyn walk up the counter to retrieve their food.

"Are you seeing what I'm seeing Christopher?"

"Of course, are ya kiddin'?" Christopher answered as he watched Marilyn walk back to her booth where Debbie waited. "Well, ya know her name now—well, ya know her *first* name. I'm sure there's not more than fifty girls named Marilyn on campus. Hey--- I've got an idea. Why not post a notice in the Student Union Building that a special drawing is gonna be held for any girl whose name is Marilyn. All they need to do is register at a table and their names will be placed in a drawing for some wonderful prize. Of course, we will be at the table registering those wonderful Marilyns."

After Michael quit laughing, he said, "What a great idea, Chris. So, you and I will be sitting at the table and when the right Marilyn comes along, we will be able to get her last name. Is that the plan?"

"Yes! Correct! She walks up; you ask her for her name to register her, and there ya go!" Chris answered with cockiness.

"And what if she doesn't come? Like she thinks the whole idea is kind of lame?" Michael asks.

"That's the one glitch----but if we have a good enough prize, that should encourage more to come," Chris answered trying to dig himself out of a hole.

"And what would that prize be?" Michael asked with a grin on his face.

16

"Haven't gotten that far, yet. Hmmm---maybe a date with us?" Chris answered shyly.

"Talk about running the other way! A date with us wouldn't even attract Minnie Mouse. Hate to tell ya that. Don't take it personally." Michael said.

"Ok----scratch that. Why not go to your friend in the registrar's office? Convince him to run the names of the freshman girls named Marilyn. At least that will narrow the list down," Chris suggested.

"Ya know what I'm gonna do?" Michael said. "I'm gonna walk right up to her and introduce myself."

"I think that is the most logical thing to do," Chris answered. "OK--get ready---get set---GO!"

"Well, OK, wait a minute. I'll go in just a second. Let me think about this. I don't want to act ridiculous. I need to be cool---ya know?" Michael was starting to get cold feet. "Let's go together."

They stood up, walked to the booth in the back where the girls were sitting and Michael said, "Excuse us, we don't want to interrupt your dinner, but we want to introduce ourselves to you. I'm Michael Moran and this is Christopher Gibbon. We've seen y'all a couple of times. Are y'all new students to the university or have you been here before?"

"Nice meeting you," Marilyn said smiling. "I'm Marilyn Johnson and this is Debbie Oats. Yes, can you tell we are freshmen? Does it show?"

"I have to admit the biggest clue was the fact that y'all were standing in the freshman line at registration," Michael said and then they laughed so loudly everyone in the restaurant heard them. "Why don't we meet here again next Friday? By that time, y'all will have been to all of your classes and ya might have some questions about the university that we can help you with. We're both juniors so we've been around awhile. There are a lot of interesting things we can tell ya about this university---and the community---and the faculty--- ya know—interesting things," Chris asked.

"That's a deal," the girls said simultaneously. "See ya Friday night."

The boys turned and walked back to their booth to finish their food. The girls walked past them on the way out, waving good-bye.

"Victory!" Michael exclaimed under his breath.

"Ok, Michael. See, that wasn't so bad after all, was it?" Chris said wanting to take a little credit for meeting the girls.

"It was great. But we have a lot of work to do," Michael said. "We have to get Marilyn's schedule from my friend in the office. I have a plan up my sleeve." Chris just looked at Michael wondering what he was up to. Whatever it was, it was sure to be exciting.

Chapter Four
Surprise Encounters

The semester was getting underway and the hustle and bustle of moving in calmed to a regular routine for everyone. The weather was beautiful---not too hot and not too cool. It was perfect for walking between classes and even in the evening after the sun sat in the horizon.

Michael managed to get Marilyn's schedule and he mapped out where her classes were compared to his. He knew where and when she would be in class. He wanted to surprise her with little things without her thinking he was stalking her. He had to be very careful; he didn't want to scare her away.

He ran down to the campus store and bought an entire sack full of miniature M&M packages. Arriving back in his dorm room, Michael told Chris what he was going to do with the candy. "See this candy? Don't you love it? Haven't you eaten them your entire life?"

"Sure. I love the chocolate center covered with a hard candy coating that melts in your mouth and not in your hand. Is this a commercial or something for M&M's? Why are ya asking?" Christopher asked genuinely interested and quite curious.

Michael continued, "I'm gonna bet that Marilyn loves chocolate----all girls do---and I like the subtle message this is gonna send."

"What subtle message?" Chris asked. "What do you mean?"

"Look at the package----M&M's----what could this mean to you?" Michael hinted without giving too much. "M… and …...M…….Marilyn…..and ….Michael…..now do ya get it?"

"Oh! Great! How did ya ever think of that?" Chris answered laughing. "And what are ya gonna do with them?" Christopher learned a long time ago to never question Michael's creativity. Michael was always coming up with something unusual.

"My idea is to take these little packages of M&M's and get them to Marilyn at unusual times and in unusual places. We have to be creative," Michael explained. "Like, tomorrow morning, she has a class at 9:30 but my class doesn't start until 10:00. I'm gonna go to her class, stay hidden until I see that she has gone inside, then I'm gonna get someone to put this bag of M&M's on her desk. I want him or her to say, 'Someone gave me this to give to you.' If she asks, 'Who?' then tell her, 'I don't know.'

The next morning, the plan was put into action. Michael saw Marilyn walk into her class and sit close to the front close to the door. *Perfect*, Michael thought. He saw a student walk by and recruited him to put the package of M&M's on Marilyn's desk. "See that blonde sitting there? I'll give ya this dollar if you'll just put this candy on her desk and walk out," Michael told the young man. The guy didn't even miss a beat. He took the package, slipped into the room before the teacher started the lecture, and put the M&M's on Marilyn's desk.

"Someone out in the hall gave me this to give to you," the young man said and then quickly slipped out the door. Marilyn looked up and toward the door but didn't see anyone at all.

Michael handed the guy a dollar and they shook hands. Both were smiling brightly. Mission accomplished.

Then Michael was off on another mission. He only had a few minutes to do what he planned next. He ran to Marilyn's dorm, found the dorm mother, and asked her if she would please put a small package of M&M's in Marilyn's room so that she would see it when she returned from her class. The dorm mother could see the enthusiasm in Michael's voice. She gladly agreed. She took the package, climbed the stairs to the second floor and opened Marilyn's dorm room. She placed the M&M's package on the desk right where Marilyn would see it when she first came in.

After class, Marilyn walked back to her dorm and unlocked her door. She placed her purse and her books on the desk and immediately noticed the package of M&M's. *What? Who is doing this?*

22

What does this mean? she thought to herself feeling totally puzzled by the turn of events. She couldn't wait for Debbie to get there to tell her about the M&M's in her class and now the M&M's on her desk.

She barely sat down when Debbie entered the door. "Whew! I'm not used to that much walking," Debbie said slightly out of breath. "I'm not used to stairs either and they are everywhere!"

"Hey Debbie---catch your breath---but listen to what happened to me today! I just entered my class and sat down when a young guy walks in and sets a small package of M&M's on my desk. He said it was from someone out in the hall and he left."

"Did you jump up and run out to the hall?" Debbie said quickly trying to ask her as fast as she could.

"No, actually I was so shocked, that I didn't even think of that. I looked out the door but couldn't see anything. I just sat there like a lump on a log," Marilyn said sadly." "Then, I get here after class and find a package of M&M's on my desk. Right here."

"Are ya kidding me? Oh, my gosh! Who did that? How did someone get into the room?" Debbie questioned. They couldn't figure it out. *Hmmm, very interesting,* Marilyn thought.

Marilyn and Debbie had another class later in the day, but they couldn't help thinking about who the mysterious person was who left the M&M's. *I'm sure we will figure this out someday,* Marilyn thought.

The next morning, both girls had to get up early to attend an 8:00 am class. This was a class they actually had together. They were excited about sharing the class and looked forward to studying together. Just as they were settling into their desks, another candy event happened. A young girl quickly walked in from the hallway, placed a package of M&M's on Marilyn's desk but said nothing and quickly walked out. This time, Debbie sprang into action and ran out the door. She glanced to the left and to the right but the mysterious girl had disappeared around the corner and out of sight. Michael knew the challenge would get more difficult, so he planned on a fast escape route. Neither he nor his accomplice were seen.

"I don't get it," Debbie said totally confused. "I moved pretty quickly, but there was no one in the hall. Not a single person." *Someone knows where I am at all times, it seems,* Marilyn thought to herself.

Nothing happened for the rest of the day and Marilyn wondered if the mysterious stranger was going to strike again the following day. She wasn't afraid----she just wondered who the person was and what was the reasoning behind the candy.

Chapter Five
Meeting at the Hamburger Place

The semester had gotten off to a great start. Both girls loved the classes that they had and were especially happy about the couple of classes they shared together. They loved walking through the campus and were starting to feel more at home, knowing their way around.

Friday arrived and they were anxious to meet Michael and Christopher again at the hamburger place. They had not seen them since the last time, so their paths were not crossing during the week. The girls were anxious to find out what interesting things they could find out about the university. It was going to be a fun evening.

When the girls arrived at the restaurant, the boys were already there. When the girls walked in the door, both boys stood up, welcomed them and politely pulled their chairs out for them---being the perfect gentlemen that they were.

"How have y'all been?" Michael asked sincerely. "How did you like your first week of school?"

"We loved it. We even have two classes together so that is special," Marilyn said looking to Debbie for her nod of agreement. "Do y'all like your classes?"

"Oh, yes. After you've been here as long as we've been here, you know which professors to get. We can help you with that in the future," Christopher said.

Then something really strange happened. When the waitress came over to their table to get their order, she took the orders, then reached into her pocket and pulled out a small package of M&M's and laid it on the table in front of Marilyn. She said, "This is for you from someone out in the parking lot."

Marilyn looked at Debbie and they both looked out the window to the parking lot. "Who gave you this?" Marilyn asked the waitress.

"I don't know," said the waitress.

"Was it a boy? A girl? Did you see the person?" Marilyn asked as fast as she could.

"No. I didn't see anyone. I just got a note asking me to get this to a girl in a blue blouse who would be coming in shortly with another girl with strawberry blonde hair and it was signed 'someone from the parking lot' so that is all I know," the waitress said puzzled by the whole encounter.

Michael could barely keep his composure. He sat there silently, as if he knew nothing about it. Chris did the same thing. They really got a kick out of the whole thing. The waitress pulled it off exactly like they wanted it to be done.

Marilyn and Debbie looked at each other wide-eyed. "When did ya get the note? asked Marilyn quickly.

The waitress answered, "About an hour ago."

"I didn't even know that I would be wearing this blue blouse an hour ago! I just threw it on about fifteen minutes ago!" Marilyn said completely confused.

Then Michael spoke up. "This is certainly interesting. What do you think, Marilyn? Do you have a secret admirer or something? Do you have a stalker? How did someone know you were going to wear that blue blouse even before you knew yourself?"

"I don't know *how* I could have a secret admirer. I don't even know anyone here! Marilyn answered.

"Well, you know me and Christopher, don't ya? Michael said smiling----smiling so much that Marilyn had to catch on.

"Did you---did you-----how did ya know----my schedule---the dorm room---blue blouse?" Marilyn asked with her words running together along with her thoughts running together. "Were *you* the one who did these mysterious things the last few days?"

"Let's think about this a bit. What do you think M&M stands for anyway?" Michael said with a really big, beautiful smile on his face. Marilyn had never seen him look so handsome. "Sometime things are not how they seem—remember that."

Marilyn was shocked. "Do I need to sound it out for you? Michael said. "Mmmmmmarilyn and Mmmmmichael. Get it?" Marilyn couldn't believe it. She was impressed that he had gone to so much trouble to get the message to her. She was certainly enamored with him, and now she knew that the feeling was mutual. *Life is really wonderful*, she thought.

For the rest of the evening the foursome talked about how the candy caper was planned and how it was pulled off without Marilyn knowing. Michael explained how he got the candy into her dorm room and how the other deliveries were made. He had great accomplices. The waitress actually waited until she got the go-ahead from Michael and then she wrote the note, mentioning the blue blouse, because she actually saw Marilyn in the blouse. Then they talked about other interesting things about the university. *This is going to be the greatest year ever,* thought Marilyn. Michael was thinking the same thing.

As they left the restaurant, the waitress smiled and gave them all the thumbs up signal. It certainly appeared that everyone was happy and the prank ended well with her participation.

The hamburger place became one of their favorite meeting places, since it was right off the campus and was easy to get to. They tried to keep a set date every Friday night.

The foursome met most Friday evenings and had a really good time. Sometimes they followed dinner with a walk round the campus. Sometimes they went to a movie or attended a performance on the campus. The more Marilyn was around Michael, the more she liked him. In fact, it wasn't just 'like' anymore. She was enamored with him and thought she was falling in love with him. *Time will tell*, she thought to herself.

Chapter Six
Relationship Blossoms

Fall was approaching. The weather turned a little cooler and some of the trees were starting to turn colors. The bright green turned to a yellow and orange with some trees displaying a bright red hue. The campus looked absolutely beautiful. The walks between classes and across campus were pleasant; the cooler air was welcomed.

Michael kept up his candy capers about once a week. He didn't want Marilyn to forget about what M&M stood for. He didn't have to rely on accomplices to deliver the candy; he just handled it himself. It was nothing for him to appear in Marilyn's class before the class started and place a package on her desk, smile, and walk out. Nothing more was said---didn't need to be.

Once, he appeared in her dorm cafeteria as she and Debbie were having breakfast. He casually walked by her table, set the package of M&M's in her lunch tray and kept walking. Just when he got to the door on his way out, he turned around and smiled at her and waved. Of course, he knew she would be watching his every step.

"Debbie, we *have* to think of something to do to Michael. This just can't be a one-way street. But, it has to be clever---really clever. Be thinking," Marilyn said as she pondered what to do. Both girls knew that they had to get to class, but their minds wouldn't be on the lesson---it would be on what to do to Michael to surprise him.

2

Later that week, Michael asked Marilyn to go with him to a family dinner. His parents were going to be in town, and they wanted to have dinner together. Michael was excited to show Marilyn off to his parents. He knew they would love her. She graciously accepted the invitation and started thinking about what she might wear.

The dinner went very well with wonderful conversation and much laughter. Michael told them his elaborate candy scheme and how he solicited help to pull it off. Marilyn explained her total confusion during the candy caper. Mr. and Mrs. Moran thanked Marilyn profusely for keeping Michael in line and for being such a good sport. They invited her to visit them in Denver, with or without Michael. "Don't let his busy schedule get in the way of a great visit---just come without him!" Mr. Moran exclaimed. "Now that we've met you, we don't really need him to come." Laughter filled the room. Michael looked at Marilyn with eyebrows raised.

He could tell his parents really enjoyed their time with Marilyn, and it made his heart full of good feelings. He was falling in love with Marilyn.

When he walked her back to the dorm, he hugged her tightly before letting her go through the door. He really didn't want to let her go, but he had no choice. "Marilyn, I had the greatest time tonight. My parents loved you. Thanks for going with me."

"The pleasure was all mine, Michael. I enjoyed your parents *so* much. But what would I expect?--nice parents---nice son. But, to tell the truth---I might just take them up on that visit---without you, of course," she said jokingly. With that comment, he grabbed her around the waist and swung her around him as he held onto her tightly.

"No, you don't! Never without me!!" he said sternly but with a huge smile on his face. "In fact, I'm not letting you out of my sight!"

Marilyn love every minute of the exchange. She loved every minute of being with Michael. She loved every minute of thinking about him. She loved every minute of -----her life.

3

"Michael, Thanksgiving is right around the corner. Do you usually go home for Thanksgiving and again on Christmas or what?" Marilyn asked.

"No, we get out so early for Christmas break that it doesn't seem that important to go home for Thanksgiving. I mean, I love my parents, but I don't want them to pay for two airline tickets that close together. I usually hang out here at the university and I get ready for final exams. What are your plans, Marilyn?" he responded.

"I'm pretty close---only a couple of hours away so my parents really expect me to be there. Why don't you come home with me? I want you to meet my parents, and that would be the perfect time. You can also meet my younger sister, Brenda." she asked already knowing the answer to her question.

"Do you think you can stand me for that long? We've never been together than much---ever!" he kidded.

"You're right---I don't know *what* I was thinking! I couldn't possibly stand seeing you for about three or four days straight. I must have lost my mind! Come to think about it, it would totally ruin my Thanksgiving. Thanks for pointing that out!" Marilyn said acting seriously.

"You are bad---you are *so* bad," he replied. Then he hugged her longer than ever before. She floated on clouds the rest of the day.

4

With as busy as everyone was with classes, tests, and projects, Thanksgiving break came quickly. Michael and Marilyn finished up their classes, packed their suitcases and jumped in the car to drive to her parents' house. Mr. and Mrs. Johnson were excited to meet Michael. Marilyn was a little shy in high school and she really didn't date much. There wasn't anyone that she really cared about in more than a friendship way, so this was really going to be different. They welcomed meeting the young man who captured Marilyn's heart like he obviously had.

Marilyn's father took to Michael right away. They started talking about golf when Michael and Marilyn arrived and didn't quit. Every time they sat down to breakfast or lunch or dinner, the topic was golf. She was thrilled that her father enjoyed talking to Michel so much, but Marilyn had to 'steal' Michael away just to spend time with him.

One evening, Michael and Marilyn got in the car and drove around town. He had never been to her home town and was curious about her old stomping grounds. She showed him the 'drag' which was the two-mile long street that ran from the town square at one end to the Dairy Queen at the other end of town. Usually every evening but certainly on the weekend, all the teenagers in town would 'cruise the drag.' Then, after driving around for a while, kids would park on the square, get out of their cars, and visit with everyone who was there. At the Dairy Queen end, everyone drove around the building before getting back on the street to go back to the square. That way, the kids could check out who was in the Dairy Queen. The town square and the Dairy Queen were certainly social, hang-out places.

Marilyn showed Michael the Eblen Pharmacy---zthe pharmacy owned by her best friend's father when they were in junior high school and high school. As young girls, they would walk to the restaurant across the street from her father's pharmacy where they would get banana splits at least every Saturday. They only cost fifty cents back in those days.

"You must actually be much older than I thought you were if you were able to get banana splits for fifty cents!" Michael joked. "Are you keeping something from me? Like your age? Man! I would have *never* thought you were any older than sixty!"

"Things are not always what they seem. Remember that," she repeated from an earlier conversation. They laughed. They did a lot of laughing during their time together.

5

Thanksgiving was being held at the Johnson house this year. It rotated among Marilyn's aunts and uncles. That meant Marilyn would be helping her mother with everything to make sure the meal was perfect. She had done it many times before.

"Mrs. Johnson, are you sure that Marilyn can cook? I don't want her part of the dinner to be a flop. Do I need to help? I've never cooked Thanksgiving dinner before, but I'm sure I can do it. What does an oven look like anyways?" he said trying to appear concerned.

"Somehow, I bet we can handle it without you, Michael. Why don't you just busy yourself with a conversation with her dad? Like something y'all haven't talked about----like golf!" Mrs. Johnson joked as she moved him out of the kitchen into the connecting family room where Mr. Johnson was sitting---watching what else? Golf.

Sitting next to her father, Michael said, "They said they don't need my help. Can you believe that?"

Marilyn enjoyed the joking back and forth. Everything just felt *so* good. Everyone was happy-- the ladies were in the kitchen preparing the meal--- and the guys were watching golf on the television. And the next exciting thing was going to be Marilyn's sister coming in. She was away on a trip when the kids came in, but she was expected to arrive any minute.

"Did you warn Michael about Brenda?" Mrs. Johnson asked her daughter. "I mean, did you explain how she likes to play jokes and such?"

"No, actually I decided to just let it play out. Let's watch how Michael handles her," she answered. "This could be very interesting."

Just as they were discussing the issue, Brenda walked through the door.

"Hey guys! I'm hhhooooommmme! Aren't you glad? Brenda yelled out as she entered the family room. Noticing Michael, Brenda walked over to her father, and whispered in his ear loudly enough for everyone to hear, "Dad, do you know there is a *very strange* man in the room?"

"Brenda," her father said, "This is Michael Moran, a very good friend of Marilyn's. They attend the university together."

"Michael Moran----Michael Moran---where have I seen that name?" she said. "Oh my gosh! I remember now! I thought I recognized you! Your picture is in the post office---on a Most Wanted poster! I think you are a robber and a murderer! So, hey---how's business? Robbed a bank lately? Need an accomplice? I could use a job right about now."

Everyone was standing around watching the spectacle when laugher rang out. Michael laughed harder than anyone. "I have an application that you have to fill out if you want to work with me," he answered. "Do you have any experience----I mean robbing banks?" he asked.

"I don't have any experience robbing banks, but they have had plenty of experience robbing me! I've paid more over-draft fees, interest on loan fees, account balance fees , and fees on more fees than you can imagine! It's robbery! I'm ready to turn the tables! Does that count?" Brenda could come up with an answer in a second.

"Hired!" Michael answered. "But first, you need to be fitted for your mask and holster. There will also be a fire arm charge, but it's minimal."

"This is going to be a very interesting Thanksgiving," Mrs. Johnson told her husband.

When Marilyn and her mother re-entered the kitchen to continue preparing the meal, Marilyn said, "Well, Mom, I think he passed the test. Don't you?"

"I certainly do!" she responded.

6

Thanksgiving Day was quite nice. All the relatives started coming over about 5:00 in the afternoon to talk and visit before the dinner meal around 6:00. Michael had the opportunity to meet all the family members in a nice, comfortable setting. He had to be on his toes at all times, however, because Brenda wasn't letting up much.

At the end of the evening, after everyone had left, Marilyn had time to sit down with Michael. They both agreed that they had more fun this Thanksgiving than any other one---ever.

"Let's have many, many more. OK?" Michael asked Marilyn then hugged her tightly.

"Promise?" she responded.

Chapter Seven
End of Semester Approaching

Thanksgiving was *so* much fun, but it was time to head back to the university and hit the books again. Marilyn couldn't wait to see her roommate, Debbie, and tell her all about Thanksgiving with Michael and her family.

Debbie had a great time during her break also, but it didn't compare to Marilyn's. Debbie was mesmerized as Marilyn told her play-by-play of what happened when Brenda got home. They laughed until tears streamed down their faces.

"We only have two and one-half weeks before we're out for the end of the semester," Debbie reminded her. "We have to figure out something like the candy caper for Michael. Have you come up with anything creative?"

"No! I haven't had time to think about it. Come on----put your thinking cap on! You can do it! We can do it!" Marilyn yelled like a cheerleader.

"OK, I have an idea," Debbie said. "Can we get to his books? What if we found out what page his assignment will be on, then put an empty M&M's bag on that page. He wouldn't notice it until he got to that page. Then he'd be surprised—right in class."

"That's a great idea! He wouldn't suspect a thing---then surprise! And it doesn't matter that we take the candy out. It's the M&M's package that says everything. He'll never suspect anything in his book!" Marilyn said giggling. "We need to recruit Christopher. He can find his syllabus and set the whole thing up in their dorm room. He may even know where Michael stashes his M&M's supply. We need Christopher!"

"One of my classes was cancelled for tomorrow, so I'll manage to meet with Christopher and get him on board. It would be great to get empty packages in several of his class books, wouldn't it!" Debbie plotted.

2

Christopher couldn't wait to get in on the fun. He knew exactly what to do. He knew what books to set up right before Michael left for class and what books to wait on. Then Chris did something special. He knew one of Michael's professors.

Michael walked into his Advanced Math and Statistics class, sat down and waited for the professor to enter. "Class, open your books to page 311 please. Let's go over the problems you were assigned last class," the professor said. Michael opened his book to page 311 and found the flattened M&M's package tucked into the crease. *Oh my gosh---that girl. She's amazing,* he thought to himself, not able to keep from smiling. He couldn't even think of anything other than Marilyn. He didn't even hear what the professor was saying. The class came to an end and he floated out of the door.

His next class was in the building next door. It was in an auditorium style lecture hall and Michael always sat about ten rows up in the middle. The professor entered the room and told the students what the lecture was going to be. He picked up a white envelope and walked up the aisle to where Michael was sitting. As he talked to the class, he handed Michael the envelope, never missing a word. Michael wondered what it was. He had never seen a professor hand a student an envelope before. *What is this?* he wondered.

Michael opened the envelope. Then he saw what was inside---a dark brown M&M's package flattened. He didn't take it out. He just grinned and slipped it into his book. *That's good---that's really good.*

When he got back to his dorm, he called Marilyn. "That's good, Marilyn. That's really good. You did it," Michael said sincerely.

"Did what?" she asked.

"You won my heart. Completely. See ya tomorrow evening."

Chapter Eight
Semester Break Apart

Marilyn and Michael decided that they would return to their separate homes for the break between semesters. It meant they would be separated for Christmas, but they could at least call each other.

It was getting so much colder. The winter winds were stronger and whistled through the trees making a very eerie sound. Maybe the chill was a preview of how Marilyn was going to feel without Michael around. She thought back to how much fun they had at Thanksgiving. She had such fond memories of that time.

Michael felt the same way. Although he hadn't seen his family since September, and he was anxious to see everybody, he couldn't help but think about what a wonderful time he had with Marilyn's family at Thanksgiving. He was going to miss the bantering with Brenda. But he was *really* going to miss Marilyn. *Can I make it a month? I won't be seeing Marilyn for a month!*

2

Michael arrived home and was greeted wholeheartedly by his mom and dad. They were ecstatic to see him. After all, they hadn't seen him since that dinner they had with him and Marilyn after the fall semester started. That was early

September—nearly four months ago. It was going to be a small Christmas at the Moran household this year. Several of their family members were out-of-town this year. Michael spent valuable time with his mother and father and was thankful he had that time with them. He helped them do things around the house, run errands, and did a lot of the cooking for his mother. His parents knew his missed Marilyn, and they could see his sadness even though he was making a good appearance around them. Then one morning when they were talking about Marilyn and all the fun things the kids did together, his mother said, "Michael, why don't you surprise Marilyn---really surprise Marilyn---by showing up at her house on Christmas Day?"

"Now you're getting in on the surprises?" Michael responded. "Are you serious? You wouldn't mind?"

"I wouldn't bring it up, if I didn't think it would be a great idea!" his mother said sincerely.

"Go for it, Son," his dad chimed in.

Michael couldn't be happier. In fact, he was so excited, he couldn't sleep at night. *This is really going to be great. I'd better call Mrs. Johnson and make sure it will OK for me to show up.*

Michael called Mrs. Johnson. She was excited about the Christmas surprise! "Wait 'til I tell her father! He's gonna love this!" she said thrilled at the thought. "Let's plan how you're going to make your entrance. Be thinking Michael---then let me know," she said.

After another conversation, they both decided that Michael would fly in, get a cab to their house, and then walk in the front door just as they were gathering around to open presents. It was a family tradition to open gifts Christmas Eve night after dinner.

So, Michael did just that. He flew in-----he was so excited he didn't need the airplane. He was flying without it. Then he grabbed a cab and in just a short time was at the Johnson' house.

When Michael arrived at the house, he was able to look through the front windows into the living room where everyone was gathered. People were sitting everywhere; some were sitting on the floor. Michael could see everything. Then when he thought it was just the right time, he opened the front door, said "Ho—ho—ho" in a deep voice and then walked into the room. What *no one* knew—not even Marilyn's parents--- was that Michael was going to walk in dressed in a complete Santa outfit including long, white beard and mustache. He walked into the room in his full costume and was totally unrecognizable to Marilyn. She thought it was just some stranger dressed up like Santa to give someone a gift as a surprise. She wouldn't put it past her uncle to hire someone to surprise his daughter.

Michael stood there waving to everyone in the room. Then he walked over to Marilyn and looked right into her eyes. She looked into his eyes and there was an electrical feeling between them. *Michael?* She thought to herself not really believing it. Then he pulled off his beard and mustache. Marilyn screamed and threw her arms around him. Everyone applauded. It was magical. It was really magical. Marilyn was the happiest girl in the whole universe at that moment.

"Michael, you'll never be able to top that one. Never," she said hugging him again.

Chapter Nine
End of Break—Back to School

All good things must come to an end. Michael and Marilyn had a great time over the break. Michael was able to stay with Marilyn and her parents for a few days before it was time for him to fly home to spend the last few days with his parents.

On the day after Christmas, a beautiful snow fell and covered the landscape. It was, indeed, a winter wonderland. It was too pretty to stay indoors, so Marilyn and Michael bundled up in coats, hats, and mittens and headed out the door. They couldn't resist the chance to build a snowman. Rolling the snow to form the body and head, Marilyn helped Michael pick up the balls to form the snowman. Just as they were looking around for something to use for the snowman's eyes and mouth, Mrs. Johnson came out of the house with unshelled pecans and a carrot. She also brought an old hat and a scarf. She must have been watching the kids build the snowman and wanted to help them with the final steps.

"Oh, wow! Just what we needed! Thanks, Mrs. Johnson!" Michael cried out. Mrs. Johnson went back inside to retrieve the camera. She had to get a picture or actually several pictures of this! Of course, the kids really clowned it up for the camera.

They even made snow angels. Lying on their backs, these two crazy college kids made the best snow angels they could. Then they had to stand up and knock the snow of each other's backs. Michael kept hitting Marilyn on the back side, saying, "Here, let me get that snow off. Oh, here's more. *Whack!* Let me just get the last little bit! *Whack*!" After about the tenth whack, Marilyn caught on and hit him back.

When the day arrived for Michael to leave, Marilyn couldn't hide her sadness. She tried to be cheerful, but her emotions took over completely. As he turned to walk down the walkway to the plane, Marilyn broke down. He turned to wave good-bye was all he saw was Marilyn holding her hands over her face crying. That really touched his heart. He was equally sad.

It was the first time in their lives that they were anxious for the semester break to be over, so they could go back to school. In fact, they both went back a day early. Their families certainly understood.

2

It just so happened that the friend foursome was back on campus in order to meet for a Friday night gathering at the hamburger place. They talked and laughed until it was late. Marilyn couldn't wait to tell about the Santa caper. Christopher and Debbie said the Santa caper won the contest for the best one yet!

They were all ready to tackle the new semester. They were anxious to finish the second semester of the courses they started and, in some cases, they were going to be adding a single semester course. This time, no one had to solicit help to find out schedules. They freely discussed what classes they were taking and at what times. It was fun finding times between classes where they could all meet to talk and have a soft drink.

The kids worked hard, made good grades, and had fun going places together. Michael continued his candy caper from time to time when Marilyn least expected it. He kept it exciting and unexpected. Marilyn continued also. Once, she placed a package of M&M's on the bench that she knew he sat on while he waited for his statistics class to start.

One day when Marilyn walked out of her dorm, she noticed there were window washers working on her building. An idea popped into her head. She walked over to the workers and asked them if they would help her with a personal joke. She explained that she needed to get an empty M&M's package taped to a window on the second floor of the building where Michael lived.

"Sure, we'll help you with that. We will be working on that building in about three days. We need to know exactly what window on second floor and do you want it in the corner or in the middle or what?" One of the window washers asked.

"I'll tell you the exact window---I'll even draw out a little diagram for you. I think taping it to the corner of the window will make it obvious to the person inside the room but unnoticeable to anyone else. I'll get you the M&M's package and the tape to use on the window. Here's my phone number if your plans change on washing the windows. Otherwise, I'll watch for y'all and get the stuff to you," Marilyn said gratefully.

"I have to admit this is a first for us," the worker said smiling, "But, we will do it for ya."

This is gonna be sooo good. Michael's desk butts right up to the window so he can't miss it! Marilyn said to herself.

Marilyn's 'candy in the window caper' went beautifully. When Michael returned to his dorm room after class, he put his books on the desk, pulled out the chair to sit down and then looked out of the window like he did every day. It was really nice to look out over the courtyard. Then he noticed the package. *Oh, you're kidding me! Really? How in the world? These windows don't open----how did she do it?*

He couldn't wait to see Marilyn---then he decided to play a little joke on her. When they met the next day at the hamburger place, he didn't mention it. He pretended he didn't notice. That got Marilyn wondering if the window washers put it on the wrong window. She didn't think that was possible based on the diagram she drew clearly pointing out the correct window. She was puzzled.

"Did you get that essay written that you wanted to write after your class today?" Marilyn asked knowing that he would write it at his desk.

"Yeah, I wasted no time. I got in from class, sat down at my desk, and wrote the essay. I didn't want it hanging over my head this weekend," he answered quite casually. Now Marilyn was really puzzled. Michael could read it in her face. He figured the joke had gone on long enough.

"Oh, and I might mention there was an M&M's package taped to my second story window. Now, the windows washers are trying to be friends with me!" he said laughing out loud. He had figured out the window washers were the accomplices when he noticed them working on the building next door.

"Very clever, Marilyn," he said. She just smiled.

3

As the end of the semester approached, Michael and Marilyn were faced with a tough decision. If they go home for the summer, they will be apart for many weeks. If they attend summer school at the university, they can see each other almost daily, and will get more of their degree plan completed. Since both of them need to work, they can try to find a job on campus or in the surrounding area. The down side is not seeing their families much.

They discussed all the pros and cons and decided to stay on campus and attend summer school. It really boiled down to not wanting to be apart for many weeks---from the third week in May until mid-September. They headed home right after the end of the semester, spent time with their families, then enrolled for summer school. It was actually enjoyable. The classes were a little bit more relaxed and moved quickly since they attended classes everyday instead of two days a week or three days a week. In just eight weeks, one summer school session was finished. Courses listed on their degree plans were ticked off pretty rapidly.

Before they could believe it, the second semester of summer school was over and the fall semester was gearing up. Marilyn thought back to the excitement she felt when she moved to the campus for her first fall semester. A lot had happened since those days. She had met a wonderful guy, had formed many friendships, and already had a year under her belt on her degree plan. Time flies!

Chapter Ten
Relationship Continues

The relationship continued for Marilyn and Michael. They spent as much time together as they could between attending classes and studying. When Thanksgiving rolled around again, Marilyn asked to go home with her and he gladly accepted. He had so much fun the Thanksgiving before and looked forward to seeing everyone again.

As the first semester came to a close, the decision was made for Michael to spend the first part of the semester break through Christmas with his parents then join Marilyn for the remainder of the time. There would be no more Santa surprise, but they could still reminisce about it.

When Michael arrived at the airport, Marilyn was there to greet him. "Michael! I missed you so much! Christmas just wasn't the same without you this year," she exclaimed throwing her arms around his neck.

"I felt the same way, Marilyn. Now we *know* we can't spend Christmas apart ever again. Even if we have to rotate between families like most married couples I know, we will have to do that." Marilyn and Michael started talking more and more about 'married couples.' It seemed inevitable that they would get married someday.

More and more when they were together, they discussed plans for the future. "Marilyn, I love you more than you can imagine. You walked into my life fifteen months ago, and you added a new dimension to living. I'm a much happier person and I thought I was happy before! I hope I make you as happy as you make me," he said sincerely.

"Michael," Marilyn started looking into his dark brown eyes. "I love every minute that I'm with you, and I think about you every minute that I'm not with you. I love you too, Michael. I don't ever want this feeling to stop. I know I have to finish my degree and I know this is your last year here, but we have to figure out a way that we can still be together. Being apart is just too difficult."

"You definitely need to finish your degree and I basically promised your parents that would happen. I'll know pretty soon if I get a job here after I graduate or if I'll have to relocate. Even if I have to relocate, maybe you could transfer to a university close to me. Let's not worry about that right now. It's still a long way off," Michael said. He also knew he wanted to marry her as soon as he graduated, so he needed to start discussing that with her soon.

On one of their dates, they walked past a church where a wedding had just taken place. They saw the bride and groom and all of the attendants outside having their pictures made. Walking past them, Michael said, "Marilyn, what kind of wedding have you always dreamed of?"

"Oh, not a big one. I've always thought of my wedding as being smaller and more intimate. I would want just one bridesmaid and one flower girl. I don't want it in a big church but maybe a small chapel or an outdoor wedding in a beautiful setting. I've always wanted a white or cream-colored dress with long sleeves made out of lace. I'm not thinking about a veil, but I often think of the bouquet. I'd like it to be made out of pink and white roses with long pink and white satin ribbons hanging down. I picture throwing the bouquet over my shoulder to my girlfriends behind me--- the ribbons streaming through the air as it is tossed."

"What kind of ring is the ring of your dreams?" Michael asked sincerely.

"Ya know, I think simple, matching gold bands would make me the happiest. I'm not one for large diamonds or too much sparkle. I'd love a simple, gold band. I really want matching bride and groom bands, maybe a quarter of an inch wide," she said getting excited at the mere thought of getting married.

They continued past the wedding party and down the sidewalk to a candy shop. They could smell hot fudge being spread on the marble table to cool and shape. "Oh, my! We can't just walk past. Not with it smelling as good as it does! Let's go in," Michael said enthusiastically. Chocolate fudge was one of Marilyn's favorites and he knew it. It reminded her of the time when her family took a trip to Mackinac Island in the Great Lakes area. Every other shop in this quaint little village is a fudge shop and they ship fudge all over the world. Tourists walk from one shop with the smell of hot peanut butter fudge to another with the smell of hot milk chocolate fudge. It's amazing…..and delicious!! Another interesting thing about the island is that there are no cars—only emergency vehicles. Everyone walks or rides in horse-drawn buggies. Then, when winter approaches, barges carry all of the horses south where they will be protected and will stay throughout the harsh, cold winters.

The end of the evening came; Michael got Marilyn back to the dorm, and he went back to his room. Marilyn replayed the conversation over and over again about wedding plans. She knew that when Michael proposed to her, it would be really amazing and very unique. There's no way she could guess what he was going to do. She'd just have to wait. That was going to be later anyway, maybe in the summer.

Chapter Eleven
Unexpected Catastrophe

The end of the school year was coming to a close. Marilyn couldn't believe her second year of college was almost over. Michael was completing his last year, and he was getting excited about starting a new job and getting on with his life with Marilyn. He just didn't know what the job was going to be or where he was going to end up. He didn't want to disrupt her degree plan and certainly wanted her to finish, but at the same time, he didn't want to move anywhere for a new job without her.

In May, Michael was busy completing his degree and interviewing for jobs. He hoped to be hired in the field of information technology, so he could end up anywhere! He traveled quite a bit to the surrounding cities, but also caught flights to companies farther away. It was hard for Marilyn to keep up with everywhere he was going and she missed not seeing him as much as usual. She knew it would be short-lived. As soon as he found the right job, they could start planning----planning on where they would live----planning on where she would attend school----planning on a wedding. So much to think about! She was so excited that she could barely keep her mind on her studies.

Marilyn's mother needed to travel to a city not too far away but wanted Marilyn to join her if she could. It would be a day trip but would be a great time to discuss the possibilities of all the things that might be happening in Marilyn's life. Marilyn wanted to discuss the possibility of transferring to another university if necessary and even plans for a small wedding. A road trip would be the perfect time to talk.

Then something terrible happened. Marilyn and her other stopped at a restaurant in Midland to grab lunch before finishing their day. They walked in, were seated near the window, and were handed menus. When Marilyn glanced around the restaurant, she saw Michael seated in a booth with a young woman. He obviously didn't see Marilyn and her mother enter the restaurant or he would have gotten up. Instead, Marilyn stopped herself from jumping up to say hello when she saw that they were holding hands. Her mother had her back to them so she saw nothing. At first, Marilyn thought that Michael might be in an interview or some kind of meeting but then the whole scene just didn't look right. He was holding the young girl's hand! They just seemed too friendly and warm toward each other. Then Marilyn saw Michael pull a box from his jacket pocket and give it to the girl. She opened the box, pulled out a necklace and immediately jumped up to hug him. Then they kissed! Marilyn's heart sank. She had a feeling of total devastation. *How am I going to tell my mother?* She thought to herself. *How is this possible?* Tears started streaming down her face.

"Marilyn! What's the matter, darling? What's the matter!" her mother said with great concern.

"Mom, I'm sorry. I don't know what's happening. I just saw Michael. He's with a girl," Marilyn managed to get out.

"Well, that doesn't necessarily mean anything, Marilyn. There's a million reasons why he might be with a girl. Where did you see him?" her mother managed to say calmly.

"You don't understand, Mom. I saw him right over there----don't look, yet. He was holding her hand. He gave her a necklace and she kissed him," Marilyn managed to get out without crying harder.

"What if she is his cousin or niece or something, and he gave her a birthday present or a graduation present or something and she kisscd him to show appreciation?" Marilyn's mother was trying to think of any scenario that would possibly be an excuse.

"Mom, *they* kissed. It wasn't her kissing him---*they* kissed. She's not his cousin. I can tell you that! Marilyn said sniffling. "They are still over there in that booth."

With that, Marilyn's mother looked toward the booth and was aghast. She couldn't believe it. It was definitely Michael. He was definitely with a young girl and they were definitely not 'just friends.' At that instant, she could feel Marilyn's pain. She could feel her heart break.

I guess things aren't always the way they seem, she thought to herself. *Maybe Michael isn't in love with me, after all.*

Her mother just had to take another good look. She couldn't believe that Michael hadn't seen them entering the restaurant or even when they were seated. Everybody glances around no matter where they are. *Maybe he was just enamored with his little girlfriend that he didn't see anything or anybody else,* she thought.

"Mom, we have to get out of here. I've got to leave. Can we go now? We haven't ordered yet," Marilyn begged.

"Of course, darling. I'm with you. Let's just leave."

They got up and walked toward the door. Marilyn didn't look back, but her mother just *had* to. She glanced back at the booth where Michael was sitting. He looked up and their eyes met. He didn't even act shocked at seeing her. She turned and walked out the door.

When they reached the car, Marilyn couldn't contain herself anymore. She broke down crying--- sobbing. Her heart was broken. Her mother was equally as sad at seeing the pain her daughter was going through.

I'm just not believing this. Michael was so enamored with Marilyn. They were the perfect couple. There were absolutely no signs of anything like this. This is crazy! Marilyn's mother thought to herself.

Marilyn just continued to cry.

"Marilyn, do you think you should confront him with this? I mean, to get an explanation?" her mom asked.

"No, Mom, I can't. I can't call him. I know what I saw. I know what was happening," she said crying between words. "I just can't believe it." Marilyn had just spent the trip telling her mother how much she loved Michael and all the discussions they had on their life together. *This is why this doesn't make sense,* thought Marilyn to herself.

The trip home was extremely long. Most of the time, no one talked. Both women were thinking, but not much talking was being done. Marilyn was still in a state of shock. When she finally spoke, she told her mother than she didn't see how she could continue at the university. "Mom, I only have a few days left and then there are finals. I'm going to ask my professors if I can take my finals in the learning center. I just *can't* accidentally run into Michael."

"Are ya gonna miss the last class or two in each course?" Marilyn's mother asked.

"Yeah, I can do that. My grades are really good right now and I won't be missing much at all. It's mostly gonna be a review for the finals. I'm pretty sure they'll let me take my finals in the learning center. Then, I'm guaranteed to never run into Michael," Marilyn said convincingly. "Mom, I don't even want to face my roommate, Debbie. I just don't want to talk about this. I know you think I am running away from this and you're right. I just can't handle this emotionally right now. Let me work through this in my own way, please."

Marilyn's mother knew she needed to let her work through her sorrow in her own way. She knew Marilyn would be OK, but it was going to take a lot of time. All she could think of was getting Marilyn through the semester and back home where she could try to keep Marilyn busy.

Chapter Twelve
Michael's Concerns

Michael knew Marilyn had gone with her mother to Midland on a short, day trip for business. He thought it was a great idea and he knew Marilyn would have time to discuss all kinds of things with her mother.

He hadn't seen much of Marilyn lately because of all of the interviews scheduled for him. He was completing his semester, too, and finishing up his courses in preparation for graduation. He wasn't worried about Marilyn, because their relationship was as solid as it could be---or so he thought.

Michael hadn't heard from Marilyn the day after the trip, so he decided to give her a call. There was no answer. Finally, Debbie answered in the dorm room. "Hello?" she answered.

"Debbie, is Marilyn there? I know she got back last night, but I haven't heard from her. That is so unlike her," he said concerned.

"Well, she's not here, and I really was expecting her last night, but she didn't come in. I just figured she and her mother decided to stay overnight. I really never worried until now that you are telling me you haven't heard from her either. Did you try calling her parents?" Debbie asked.

"Not yet, but I'll do that. Thanks anyway, Deb. If she does come in, would you please tell her to call me?" he asked.

"I'll do it!" Debbie responded.

Michael hung up the phone and immediately called the Johnson's home phone. It rang and rang with no answer. *That is really strange*, Michael thought to himself. *Maybe I shouldn't be so paranoid. She was with her mother, after all. Give it a little time; Marilyn is super busy also with the end of the semester and finals.*

Michael tried to ignore the thoughts that kept popping into his head. He knew something was wrong, but he couldn't quite figure out what it was. Another day went by with no answer from Marilyn. He called her parents' home again. Again, there was no answer.

What Michael didn't know was that Marilyn was at home with her parents and that her mother turned the phone off at the answering machine. She knew it would disturb Marilyn if Michael called, so she managed to eliminate that problem. That's why the phone range, but no one answered it.

Brenda, Marilyn's sister, came to visit. She heard the whole story and was totally shocked. She tried to play down the whole thing, acknowledging the sorrow Marilyn was feeling but trying to help Marilyn understand that it just wasn't meant to be and there would certainly be many more guys out there dying to be with Marilyn. One day when Brenda was at home, she was on the phone when Michael called. She took his call not knowing he was the person on the other line.

"Brenda? Is Marilyn there? I've been so worried about her. I haven't heard from her," Michael asked somewhat relieved that he had at least gotten in contact with someone.

Brenda didn't have much time to think about her response, but she knew one thing----she didn't want Michael to talk to Marilyn. "Michael, I'm so sorry, but Marilyn has met someone else. She feels terrible, so it would be better if you wouldn't try to contact her. It would just be better with everyone."

For a couple of seconds, Michael actually thought Brenda was kidding. He remembered how she liked to joke and tease people. But, he had a different feeling about it this time. She sounded too serious. Still in a state of shock, Michael answered, "I don't understand that. I just don't understand."

"I'm sorry, Michael. You'll get past this. Be strong," Brenda told him actually feeling sorry for him but feeling mad at the same time. *It's a miracle I didn't just tell him off,* Brenda thought. *How dare he hurt my sister like that! She'll never get over this.*

Marilyn's mother told her father about what happened in the restaurant on the trip.

"I saw him with my own eyes! I wouldn't have believed it, but I saw him with my own eyes. There is no doubt. That was Michael. What Marilyn saw that I didn't see was how he and the girl were holding hands and then he gave her a necklace. Then, there was a kiss. Brannon, Marilyn saw all of that unfold in front of her eyes. Poor baby. Can you imagine the pain? Marilyn told me they were talking about getting married and were already making some plans. She was totally devastated," Mrs. Johnson explained.

"He didn't see you when you walked in?" Brannon asked.

"No, I think he was so enamored by this girl that he didn't even see anything else," she answered.

"There's got to be more to this story. I still think Marilyn should confront him. She needs to find out," Mr. Johnson said somewhat confused.

"There is no way she's going to confront him. In fact, she won't even go back to school and has already arranged to take her finals in the learning center, so she won't run into him anywhere. She can't face him," Mrs. Johnson explained.

"Well, he certainly faked us out, didn't he? I really liked him. I really did." *I guess things aren't always what they seem to be.*

Marilyn called Debbie because she knew Deb would be very worried, if she didn't hear from her.

"Debbie? This is Marilyn. I'm sorry I didn't call you sooner, but there have been some family issues I need to work through. I won't be going back to the campus, but I'll be finishing my finals next week. I'll explain all of this someday, but for now, just know that I'm working through some difficulties."

"So glad you called Marilyn! I *was* worried! Michael called hunting for you, also. He sounded worried," Debbie explained.

"I'm sorry, Debbie. I can't go into it now, but Michael will be OK. I have to handle this myself," Marilyn answered sadly.

Marilyn hung up thinking that maybe that would work for now. She couldn't talk about it. She just wanted to pretend that everything---including her pain---was going to go away.

I loved Michael so much. I thought we were the perfect couple. I'll never understand why he was with that girl. I don't understand anything about this. I had no idea. I remember him telling me one time that things aren't always how they seem. Now,

I understand what he meant by that saying---I guess.

Chapter Thirteen
Michael's New Life

Michael went into a deep depression. He loved Marilyn and wanted to spend the rest of his life with her. He knew how she felt about him, also. *How in the world could Marilyn find someone else? It doesn't even make sense,* Michael thought to himself. *But if she wanted to be with me, she would have already called. So, something definitely happened.*

Michael ran by Marilyn's classes, but she was never there. Then on the days of final exams, he went to her classes, but she wasn't there. Her roommate never saw her, either.

The job interviews resulted in several job offers. Michael had the task of deciding which job he should accept. Before Marilyn disappeared, he would have analyzed which job would be the best for the two of them---which job offer placed him in a city with a good university for Marilyn. She still had two years to complete her degree. But now, Michael felt lost. He just needed to get on with his life. He was devastated. His heart was broken.

2

Michael moved back home awaiting his move to Houston. He told his parents about the situation with Marilyn. They couldn't believe it, either. They had met Marilyn and really enjoyed her company. She was such a sweet, sincere young woman who appeared to love Michael very much. They felt so sorry for Michael. They knew the pain that he was going through and wanted it to disappear, however, they knew he would have to work through it, and it would take time. Such sorrow.

"Michael, someday you will find out why this happened. You might not know for a long time, but there may be a reason this happened to you. Things work out the way they are supposed to. Just believe that you will be fine, and you will get beyond this sorrow and disappointment," his father told him.

His parents knew that nothing they said would make him feel better right now. They knew that the new job might be the very best thing for him. He will be busy building his new career and, hopefully, will be too busy to be so sad.

Michael and his parents packed up everything that he needed for his new apartment in Houston. His mother used her decorating skills to make the apartment look great. She set up his kitchen and even organized his storage closet. They really enjoyed working with Michael on setting up his apartment, and he seemed to be adjusting well to his new location.

His first day on the job was fantastic. Everyone there welcomed him royally. He was given a beautiful office and was provided with a company car. He loved his colleagues and felt that he had definitely made the right decision. There was only one thing missing----Marilyn. She was supposed to be with him wherever he landed. She should have been the one decorating the apartment. She should have been the one setting up the kitchen. His heart was still broken.

Immediately, his friends and colleagues wanted to set him up with the beautiful, single girls that they knew. After all, he was extremely handsome, was brilliant, and was beginning a fantastic career. He was one of the most eligible bachelors in the area. When his friends tried to set him up, he always had an excuse to get out of it. He just couldn't go out yet. He was still grieving the fact that he lost Marilyn and never really understood why. He knew what her sister told him, but he could never understand how that could have happened. He just needed time.

Michael threw all of his energy into doing his job. He arrived in the office early and was the last one to leave in the evening. He generated more business than anyone else. He appeared to be a super star, but he did it to cover up his sadness. He tried to work himself out of loneliness and sadness and depression.

In no time at all, Michael was promoted to assistant vice president which required more travel and more responsibility. He accepted his new position graciously.

4

Michael kept climbing in his company. He was so busy, that he didn't have time to think about anything else. His friends quit trying to set him up with dates, because they knew he was on the go so much. When he was at home, he just wanted to relax and regroup. He certainly wasn't into entertaining and making small talk with someone he didn't know.

Almost five years went by with Michael working every minute he could work. He got away, every once in a while, to spend time with his parents; he knew they were getting older and he wanted to help them whenever possible. Maybe it was a psychological issue that Michael didn't want to have another relationship.

Then really unusual things started happening.

Chapter Fourteen
Mistaken Identity

One day, Michael was required to attend a meeting in Midland for the company. When he arrived at the airport and walked to the rental car place, the attendant there surprised him.

"Hi Dean! Hey, it's good seein' ya again," the attendant said cheerfully.

"Oh, I'm sorry. I'm not Dean. I'm Michael Moran from Houston," Michael replied thinking it was a little strange he was mistaken for someone else.

"Well, you look exactly like him---that's all I have to say. Thanks for choosing Fast Car Rental," the attendant said smiling.

Michael filled out the paperwork, picked up the keys and headed for the car. *That was strange*, he thought.

The meeting went well and Michael was his way back to Houston that evening. Houston was really feeling like home to him, and he had to admit to himself that he didn't think about Marilyn everyday like he once did. He still thought of her, though, and it made him sad.

The time finally came when Michael agreed to meet on a double date with one of his best friends. They decided to go out to dinner and then catch the musical being performed at the local theater center. Michael caught himself getting dressed for the date but wondering to himself what he thought Marilyn might like to see him wear. *Why am I doing this? This is crazy. Marilyn is gone---long gone---never to return. Get over it.*

The foursome met at the restaurant; his friend Noah picked up not only his girlfriend, but the girl that Michael was supposed to meet, also. They were close friends, after all. The three of them were already in the restaurant when Michael walked in the door.

Michael looked stunning. He wore black slacks with a cream-colored sweater. He wore his best black lizard cowboy boots, not because they were very handsome, but that they were very comfortable. His black hair was styled perfectly and his face was slightly tanned. His chiseled facial features were typical of the male model seen in all of the fashion magazines. He complimented himself on actually going out on a date. He saw that as a step forward in his healing process. He couldn't believe the years had passed---more than ten years since graduation.

The dinner went very well. Michael proved that he was not only one of the most handsome men in the restaurant, but also one of the most delightful. Stella, the girl introduced to Michael, was mesmerized. She couldn't believe such a wonderful man could stay single for so many years! The four friends had a great time at dinner and then the musical proved to be quite entertaining. Michael sat next to Stella and then whispered to each other throughout the performance. Noah and Susie commented to each other how well Michael and Stella seemed to be getting along. They were happy that Michael appeared to be happy. They knew he had been very sad since the time they had met him, even when he tried to cover it up. They wondered what it was that caused such emotional pain, but Noah never asked. He knew Michael would tell him if and when he wanted to. It never came up.

At the end of the evening, Michael drove Stella home and walked her to her front door. "It was so nice meeting you, Stella," Michael said sincerely. "I really enjoyed our evening together and hope we can go out again sometime soon. Do you think you'd have time to go out again next week?"

Are you kidding? Stella thought before she answered. "Sure! I had a great time and would love to go out with you again. I enjoyed our conversation and laughter. I laughed more tonight than I have in the past year. How refreshing!" Stella said enthusiastically.

"I'm traveling quite a bit, but I should be back for a few days next week. I'll call you," he said.

Michael actually felt good for the first time in a long time. Stella appeared like she really liked him and wanted to spend time with him. He was still cautious because of what happened to him before, but he thought it was finally time to try a relationship again. Actually, it was *way* past time, but he could never think about anyone else until now.

Maybe his is just what I need, Michael thought to himself. *I need to get on with my life. I'm successful in my business but what's missing is a family. I'd like to someday get married, buy a home, and have children. I think it's time.*

3

While Michael was away on his trip, he had time to think about everything. When memories from the past kept surfacing, he vowed to stop thinking about them. He wanted to focus on the present. Stella was a very nice young woman and they enjoyed the time they had together. He decided to continue seeing Stella and time would tell if the relationship would work or not. *I've always heard that the magic number of months to know someone before making a permanent decision is eighteen months,* Michael thought to himself. Then he realized that he had known Marilyn a few months longer but still had no idea that she would change her mind about him. *So, there is no guarantee*, he thought.

When he returned home, he called Stella. "Stella?" he said when she answered. "This is Michael. I'm back in town and was wondering if you would like to go to dinner tomorrow evening."

"Great! I'd love to go. Hey, have you heard about that new Mexican food restaurant on Frankfurt?" she asked knowing that Mexican food was his very favorite. "Julie went there the other night and said the guacamole was the best she had ever eaten."

"OK, I'll pick you up at 6:00," he said cheerfully.

This is going to be the beginning of my life. I am going to be happy and I am going to go forward for the first time in almost ten years. Finally.

Chapter Fifteen
Marilyn's Life

Summer vacation had come to a close and the school year was just beginning. The excitement of beginning a new year was evident everywhere. The girls had their new clothes and they sported their favorite designer bags----or favorite knock-off designer bags. The boys didn't care so much about their new jeans, but they loved talking about the new cars---or new-old cars---that were pulling into the student parking lot. New backpacks and new notebooks were toted around and crammed into lockers when the combination locks worked. The freshmen were nervously looking around for their first class while the seniors were casually strolling down the hall, checking out the new kids coming into the school.

Marilyn loved every minute of it. She taught English and had taught at MacArthur High School for the past several years. She was beyond the 'early' years of teaching when teachers are trying to figure out what kind of discipline they should use and how the curriculum is going to flow. She had everything down very well and entered the years of teaching when she could finally really enjoy herself.

She enjoyed teaching literature but also enjoyed teaching her students correct grammar so that they would appear 'educated.' She knew very well that everyone uses incorrect grammar in their daily speech, and her students heard incorrect grammar on television every day. If they attended a movie, the actors used incorrect grammar. It was the same with sports announcers and news announcers. Marilyn hoped to teach them the difference so that when they entered the next grade, they would be able to write grammatically correct essays. She knew they needed correct grammar in writing their college essays for their college applications. Then, once they were accepted into the university of their choice, they would need to write grammatically correct essays for their university classes. She was on a mission.

Marilyn was so busy every day that she had very little time to think of anything else. Maybe she planned it that way, so she would not remember what had caused her so much heartache in the past. Whatever the reason, she threw herself into her profession, and soon became one of the best teachers on the faculty. Always eager to help others, she willingly took the inexperienced teachers under her wing to help them with any problems that they may have encountered.

The high school where Marilyn worked was pretty large---approximately two thousand students. It was racially proportional with approximately one-third Anglo students, one-third Hispanic students, and one-third Black students. The remainder was made up of Asian and 'other' students. She loved them all.

While at the high school, the nation experienced a wave of 'streakers.' These were individuals who, for whatever reason, decided that they should remove all of their clothing and 'streak' in front of large audiences. It was no different at her school. The word got out that a streaker would run around the practice football field adjacent to the school right before the last period of the day. Although none of the teachers or the administration got the 'memo', the students certainly did. When the bell rang to signal the five-minute passing period before last period, almost every student in the school ran to the east side of the building. If they were in a class on that side, they looked out of those windows; if they were in classes on the west side, they ran to a hallway with windows on the east side. Then, just as promised by some anonymous source, some high school student, totally nude except for a ski mask covering his face, ran around the entire practice football field. Kids screamed; kids cheered; kids giggled. Teachers shook their heads. At least it didn't last long.

On another day, approximately a year later, another incident occurred which could have been quite serious. There was one, long central hallway in the high school that had large double doors at each end. The hallway was tiled with metal lockers on either side between doors that led to classrooms. There was no previous warning on this prank, because no one seemed to know about it ahead of time.

Someone opened the double doors at one end of the hallway. An anonymous masked person on a large motorcycle drove through the hallway at full speed, causing the loud motor sound to ricochet off the metal lockers. The sound was deafening. Someone else opened the double doors at the opposite end of the hall and the motorcycle driver escaped down the street.

Most people were in a state of shock at just hearing the loud motorcycle speeding down the hallway. Luckily, no one walked out of a classroom into the hallway while this occurred. If so, a horrible accident could have occurred!

The streaker running around the football field harmed no one other than the poor freshmen who couldn't believe what was unfolding in front of their eyes. But the motorcycle fiasco? It could have actually killed someone.

Another incident that Marilyn got to witness first hand involved two girls who were fighting in the hallway. The girls were swinging their arms and were trying to slug each other. With long fingernails, they scratched each other's faces and pulled each other's hair out. Kids were surrounding them in the hall, making it more difficult for the teachers to pull them apart. When the fight was finally ended, the girls were bloody. That's when Marilyn wondered if there were such a thing as a combat duty stipend!

Once when Marilyn looked out into the hall during one of her classes, she noticed a very thick, black cloud making its way down the hall. *What in the world?* She wondered. By the time she saw it, the administrators were already on site. It turned out that someone put a roll of toilet paper between the toilet seat and the toilet, and then lit the paper on fire. As it burned, it burned the black plastic seat, sending a very thick, black cloud of smoke down the hallway. It was so thick, one could cut it with a knife. The fire alarm rang out and students filed out of the building until the smoke could be cleared.

There was never a dull moment in the high school. Then Marilyn recalled another incident. As she was giving a lecture, one of her students took a screwdriver and proceeded to remove the doorknob from the door to the classroom. The door was left open during the lecture so the doorknob was not seen from inside the class. Since Marilyn's classroom was at the end of the hallway, it was rare for anyone to walk by. No one could hear what was going on inside the classroom, either. Thus, the caper went undetected. That is, it went undetected until the perpetrator was so proud of his work that he wanted to tell his classmates—right after he did it. Marilyn calmly said, "Well, if I were you, I'd turn it back around the right way before the principal finds out." She said nothing more. He unscrewed it and turned it around the right way.

After spending several years teaching regular high school classes, Marilyn was offered a position as a resource teacher, teaching students with learning disabilities. Although she missed the large classroom setting, this new job made use of her recently acquitted master's degree in special education. She had no more than five students at a time and also had a fulltime adult teaching assistant to help. She started noticing that during one particular class period, her students were anxious to see the plants and how they were growing in the pots placed on the bookcase room divider. Marilyn always loved plants and she had plenty of containers in the room with ivy and other easy-to-raise houseplants. But these students were more interested than normal. Marilyn never let on that she knew, but she overheard the kids talking about the 'pot' that they had planted in one of the containers on the shelf. Every day, they walked it, checked out the container, and then sat down for their studies. Marilyn let it continue for a few days but when a little tiny sprig of 'pot' actually appeared one day, she worried that the word would get out that Ms. Marilyn was growing pot in her classroom. She pulled up the green twig and it was gone! When the students came in the next morning to check out their crop, they were aghast! It was gone! How could it be!

"Ms Johnson, did anyone come in here this morning?" they asked among many whispers back and forth.

"I haven't seen anyone, guys. My door was locked when I wasn't here," she answered casually. "Why? Is something wrong?"

"Nah---it's nothing. Just wondering," they answered. One could see the disappointment in their demeanor. So, that was the end to the marijuana caper.

Chapter Sixteen
Marilyn Meets Someone New

Winter Break had come and gone and now the spring semester was on its way. It was still very cold, however. Snow had fallen and made a white blanket over all of the roads and fields. The trees were a canopy of white, adding beauty to the overall landscape. Marilyn loved how everything looked. She didn't like, however, getting up so early and driving to work when it was so cold. *I'd love to just stay in my warm bed, snuggled up with my favorite blanket,* she thought. Then she'd bounce out of bed and hit the shower.

Marilyn was thankful that her life was so busy. It kept her mind off the life that she thought she was going to have with Michael. She loved teaching and enjoyed her work very much. She wasn't really interested in dating anyone until something happened at work.

On this particular day, she arrived at the school and was walking toward the door when a man took her elbow to help her over the curb, as a true gentleman would. "Here, I don't want you to slip down right in front of me. It's pretty slippery since the ice and snow," he said kindly.

"Oh, thank you so much," Marilyn said with much appreciation. She wasn't used to being helped; she was always so independent.

They introduced themselves, and then they both walked into the building and went their separate ways. "Thanks again," Marilyn called out smiling. *Boy, he sure is a nice man.* Marilyn didn't think she would ever see him again. She was wrong.

2

The bell rang for Marilyn to start her fourth period class when she noticed a man walk by her room. She thought nothing of it until he walked back by going the other direction. He looked in each time. *Is that the man who helped me over the curb today? I can't really tell.*

Then on his third pass by the open door to her classroom, he waved. *Yeah, that's the man,* she thought wondering if he needed her for anything. She walked to her door, looked out and saw him walking down the hall. He turned to look back just as Marilyn stood there watching. He just waved and kept going. *Interesting*, she thought. *And a little strange.*

She really never thought about it again, until she ran into him in the teachers' cafeteria. Marilyn was standing in line when he came up to her and asked if she would join him at his table.

"Sure, thanks," Marilyn replied to his invitation. She picked up her selections and then made her way to his table. He stood up, pulled out her chair and then seated her. *What a gentleman*, Marilyn thought. *I could get used to this.*

"Are you a teacher here?" she asked knowing she had never seen him before.

"No, I'm actually a professor at the university, but I'm here to observe some of the student teachers. You have a really good group of new student teachers," he responded delightfully.

"That's good to hear. How long will you be here?" Marilyn asked sincerely.

"For the rest of the week. Then I'll be off to another high school to observe other student teachers," he responded. He and Marilyn chatted for the rest of the lunch period and then it was time to go back to class. *He's a really nice guy*, Marilyn thought to herself. *I should find out more about who he is.*

3

Later that day, Marilyn ran into the department chairman when she turned in a report that was needed. "Virginia, do you happen to know that professor who is here observing student teachers?" she asked.

"Oh, yes. That is Dr. Richard Stratman. He has been with the university for quite some time, and he is always the one who observes the new student teachers. They all love him. He is such a gentleman. Ya know, a very sad thing happened to him a couple of years ago. He and his wife were riding in a bus that lost control and turned over. They were on a vacation in the Honduras. She died in the accident. He has never really gotten over that," Chairman Clements said.

"Oh, I'm so sorry to hear that. I can't imagine losing a spouse," Marilyn answered thinking that she almost had a spouse once, but she lost him, too. He didn't die---he just rejected her for someone else. *Quit thinking about that! Quit it! Don't even go there!*

4

Marilyn drove to school hoping that she would actually run into Dr. Stratman again. *Isn't this kind of crazy*, she asked herself. But once she got to school, she realized that she didn't even know where he was stationed while there. The school was so large that her chances of running into him would be slim. But, she remembered that he was the one who walked past her door----three times. *Maybe it will happen again.* And it did.

Just as Marilyn was preparing for her third period class, Dr. Stratman walked into her classroom. "Hello, Marilyn. I thought I'd just drop by before your class started to ask an important question."

"Sure," she said thinking he was going to ask something about her class or about the school.

"Would you go to dinner with me Saturday night? He already knew that she was single. He had checked that out already. "I thought we could compare notes on teaching and anything else that sounds really intriguing----like students or student teachers," he said laughing. "Don't you think students are intriguing?" he asked.

"Oh, absolutely, positively----have never thought any topic was as intriguing as students. Really!" she responded sarcastically. "But, the answer is 'yes.' I'd love to go to dinner with you Saturday evening."

"Great. Write your address down and I'll pick you up at 6:00. Is that a good time?" he asked.

Marilyn wrote her address on a slip of paper and handed it to Dr. Clements. She had a really good feeling about seeing him Saturday. *This is the first time in years that I have even wanted to go out with anyone. Maybe, I am finally healing. Maybe, my life is finally on track to start 'living' again.*

5

The evening was very cold. Marilyn wore one of her favorite sweaters and her favorite wool slacks. She took out her long coat and set out her cashmere scarf. She would be prepared for the cold weather.

Dr. Startman did the same. He knew the winter wind was going to make the temperature feel much colder---the chill factor was twenty degrees lower. They would be in the warm restaurant but walking to the car at her house and even at the restaurant would be chilling. Even with valet parking, they would be out in the cold for several minutes. But it was perfect. The cold gave Dr. Startman the permission to put his arm around Marilyn and hold her close----to keep her warm, of course. *This feels good,* thought Marilyn. *This feels great*, thought Dr. Stratman.

They were seated in a private booth near the back of the restaurant. The lights were slightly dim and the classical music was pleasingly pleasant but low enough to have conversation easily. Starting with a nice glass of wine, the couple talked for thirty minutes before they even ordered. Their conversation flowed easily.

"Tell me about yourself, Marilyn," Richard said. "I don't know anything other than the fact that you are highly intelligent and extremely beautiful."

"You are so nice---extremely nice---but, I think you must be talking about someone else. I don't fit that description," Marilyn said with a little giggle.

"You most certainly do. Remember, I know quite a few people at the high school where you teach, so I have already checked the intelligence thing out. On the second characteristic, I just had my eyes tested and I have perfect vision," Richard replied staring at Marilyn.

"OK, I will accept your compliments," she answered. "I really appreciate that."

The rest of the evening went well. They had a wonderful meal, another glass of wine, and talked until the restaurant was emptying out. They could tell it was time to go home. Richard walked Marilyn to the front of the restaurant and then summoned the valet parking attendant for the car. Opening the car door for Marilyn, he seated her in the car then helped move her coat so that the car door wouldn't close on it. The drive back to her house was quite pleasant and the conversation was lively. They joked and laughed a lot.

"Marilyn, I had a really good time tonight. Thank you so much for going with me," he said sincerely as he glanced her way.

"I had a great time, too. I haven't laughed this much in at least ten years. Who would have thought two educators could have such an exciting time without students around!" she answered.

When Richard walked Marilyn to her door, he put his arm around her and held her close. We have to huddle up to keep warm," he said laughing. She could see through that. She laughed, too.

She closed the door behind her. *I had a great time. I think he is a great guy. I am a lucky girl.*

Chapter Seventeen
Marilyn and Richard

Dr. Stratman completed the work he needed to do at the high school where Marilyn worked and prepared to go to next high school to observe another group of student teachers. Before he left, he walked past Marilyn's classroom and waved until he caught her attention. Her students were working on a textbook assignment, so she was free to walk out into the hallway. Richard put something in her hand.

"Marilyn, I just wanted to stop by to say 'good-bye' before I leave. I'll call you tonight and we can make plans for the weekend---that is---if you are free." Richard looked amazingly handsome in his overcoat and briefcase.

Marilyn nodded her approval and then watched as he walked down the hall. She opened her hand to see what he had given her. It was a single Hersey's candy kiss. *Oh, a kiss. I wonder if he meant anything by this or if it was just a nice gesture to give me a piece of chocolate. Hmm.*

She thought about him on and off throughout the rest of the day. She was so happy and cheerful---more than usual. She kept thinking about the candy kiss. The more she thought about it, the more she thought that he was being symbolic. *I think he meant something by giving me a 'kiss.'*

Marilyn finished the day, packed up her satchel with the papers she wanted to grade, then bundled up to face the cold walk to her car. She remembered how Richard held her tightly under the guise of keeping her warm. She wished that he were there with her at this very minute.

Later that night, Richard called Marilyn just like he said he would. He told her about the high school where he would be observing new student teachers. She told him about the answers the students gave on the textbook assignment she had to grade. High school kids are so funny when they don't know the answer to a question. They turn it into a joke and will write almost anything. They keep her laughing, that is for sure.

"I have a joke for you, Richard," Marilyn started. And what is really amazing is that I can't even tell jokes! I always mess then up, and sometimes I even forget the punch line which really messes it up. So, bear with me. Here it goes."

Students were taking a test in Mrs. Smith's classroom. When she graded the fill-in-the-blank test, she called a student up to the front to her desk. "I'm giving you a failing grade," she said. "For cheating. You copied from Jim's paper."

"I wasn't cheating," said Johnny. "Why do you say I was copying?"

"Well," his teacher continued. "On one of the blanks, Jim wrote that he didn't know the answer."

"I don't see how that shows I was copying him," Johnny answered.

"On the same test question that he answered, 'I don't know the answer,' you wrote, 'I don't either.'"

Marilyn was actually able to get the whole joke out without any glitches. They both laughed loudly over the phone.

"Hey—that was really good. You did it. Tell me another one," Richard said.

"Nope. That was it—my one joke. It will take me at least a week to practice another one. I'll let ya know when I'm ready," Marilyn joked.

The nightly phone call became regular. Richard called every night, and they talked for at least ten minutes each time. Marilyn welcomed the conversation. It was refreshing to talk to an adult after spending all of her time with teenagers at school during the day.

3

Marilyn managed to complete her doctorate while working; it had been her goal for several years. The degree enabled her to become an assistant principal and later a principal. Crazy things still happened.

When Marilyn became an assistant principal, she had another encounter with marijuana. It reminded her of the time her resource students planted marijuana in a potted----no pun intended---plant in the classroom. One day while in her office, a student came in claiming that he knew where some 'pot' was stashed across the street in a brick fence.

"Can ya take me to it?" Marilyn asked him calmly.

"Sure," he said and they headed out the front door of the school. Just across the street from the school and tucked inside an opening in the brick fence was a plastic bag with marijuana inside.

"Thanks, Jonathan. I really appreciate your telling me about this," she said patting him on the back. Marilyn took it into the principal and then carried on with her day. *It's always something*, she thought to herself. *Never a dull moment.*

One day when Marilyn got to the school, she was greeted by a teacher who told her he just came in through the front door of the school and there was a dummy hanging from the upper floor of the school right over the front door. It was made to look like a person, but no one could figure out if it were a male or female dummy. The idea was that someone was mad at the administration and wanted to show their discontent with this dummy. There was a sign with some negative reference to the administration.

Before even walking out to look at the item of such curiosity, Marilyn asked, "Does it have long eyelashes and long nails?" Marilyn wore her fingernails long and she always wore false eyelashes. She walked outside and looked at the dummy. By now, the principal was there with the campus officer, but she noticed the dummy did not have long nails or eyelashes. *Whew!* she thought to herself and went back into the building to finish her work. *What else is gonna happen today?*

A few days later something did happen. Someone let several mice loose in the commons area where all the students hang out during the lunch periods. It was a total dud. The poor mice tried to run and hide, so they were of no consequence to anyone. Most of the students in the commons area never even knew what was happening. The perpetrators thought the mice would be let loose, the students would start screaming---especially the girls---and then they would run down the hallway screaming. None of that happened.

There was also a time when students tried to get back at other students by writing mean, hateful things about them and printing flyers to distribute in the commons area. About 50 to 100 flyers would be printed with hateful messages about specific people and then they would be dropped in the commons area. Kids rushed over to pick up the flyer to see who was saying what about whom. It was like immediate gossip.

Of course, the people talked about on the flyers were devastated. Sometimes secrets they confided in others were told outright. It really was a very nasty thing to do to someone else. It happened many times, but on this one occasion, a very well respected student, clean-cut student wrote the flyer about a girlfriend who had just jilted him. The principal and assistant principals started investigating immediately. A name was given to the principal and that student was called in to the office for interrogation. He denied and denied which is exactly what every student does in every case. That is, until the student figures out there is no way out. Then, that student might confess and provide more information concerning the incident.

When 'Jack' (not his real name) was called into the interrogation, he knew things were heating up and there was probably suspicion on his part that someone had told on him. He decided to call in the big guns----his father.

Jack's father was an anesthesiologist and walked into the meeting with the principal in his green scrubs. Marilyn was also seated in the principal's office. Jack's father proceeded to explain that he was very upset about the whole incident and that the fact that we targeted his son as the perpetrator was totally ridiculous and totally out of line. Jack was also sitting in on this meeting.

"We have good reason to believe that it was your son who wrote and dropped the flyers in the commons area. We wouldn't ever investigate a student, unless we had solid reason to do so. We would never accuse a student unless we were sure about the accusation," the principal said very calmly.

With that explanation, Jack's dad got very angry and started raising his voice, "That is ridiculous! I'm gonna to have your job!" Then he looked at Marilyn and said, "I'm gonna to have *your* job, too!" Then he spoke to his son. "Jack, I want to know. Did you write that flyer? Did you do that?" Jacks father looked straight at him.

Jack looked down then said, "Yeah---I did it."

With that, the doctor stood up and stormed out of the room. There was no "Sorry" or "I won't be getting your job after all" or "Guess I made a mistake." There was nothing. Jack was allowed to go back to class and Marilyn and the principal just looked at each other. *Well, all in a day's work*, they thought.

Marilyn loved her students and teachers. They knew she really cared about them, and she would do anything for them. Above all else, she wanted to be fair. Frequently, when she had to discipline students, they would leave her office and say, "Thank you." *What kid in the world would say that*

when I just had to give him a Saturday detention?
She thought.

Because she was seen as fair, she had the trust and
respect of the students. Once when she disciplined
around eight students for doing something, one
student came back in later and said, "Dr. Johnson,
Jim was part of the group, but he really didn't do
anything wrong. He wasn't among the students
who should be punished."

Marilyn responded, "Thank you for telling me that.
I trust what you say. I would never want to punish
anyone for doing something he didn't do. If you say
he is innocent, I will believe you."

The irony is that when Marilyn became the
principal of the middle school, she always attended
the athletic games afterschool in the gymnasium.
One day when the eighth-grade girls were playing
volleyball, Marilyn stood on the sidelines watching
the game. The doctor, Jack's father, appeared
alongside her. He acted like they had been friends
forever.

Then another ironic thing happened. Marilyn had to
have a minor medical procedure one day and after
the doctor described what he was going to do, he
said, "Your anesthesiologist will be here in just a
minute. He is really good. His name is Dr. Eric
Johnson." *Oh my gosh*---thought Marilyn. *That's
Jack's dad! Oh well, I guess we are old friends by
now.* She didn't know if he would remember her at

all, but she figured he probably would. He did. Actually, it was a nice reunion of sorts.

Chapter Eighteen
A Change of Plans

Marilyn and Richard enjoyed talking on the phone every night, commiserating about the days' events and getting together on the weekend for dinner very often. They had so much in common. Then one Saturday evening over dinner, Richard gave Marilyn some news that was a little disheartening.

"Marilyn, I have been given the opportunity to take a huge advancement in my career. I didn't seek this out; instead, they contacted me. I have been asked to become the Dean of the College of Education at Harvard University. I really never expected anything like this to happen. They have officially offered me the job and now they are just waiting for my answer. We are negotiating the salary and benefits now," Richard said with mixed emotions.

"Oh, wow!" Marilyn tried to sound enthusiastic but inside she felt sadness inching into her thoughts. "That's marvelous! Harvard of all places! Of course, you have to take it. What are you waiting on?"

'Well, I agree with you. This is an opportunity of a lifetime, so I feel I must take it. I'm just saddened by the fact that I enjoy being with you so much and now we'll be apart----that is, unless you want to go with me," he said smiling. "I know you've worked your way up in the administration where you are now, so I don't know how you'd feel about leaving that. You don't have to answer right now---think about it over the next few days. We can talk about it."

"I know---I have very mixed emotions about your leaving. I can't see myself leaving my position and starting over somewhere else, and particularly not leaving without having a job in place. We have enjoyed each other's company----at least I think I can talk for both of us----or maybe not?" She laughed then continued. "But, our relationship is still pretty new, so we'd need to give each other more time anyway."

"We can certainly continue talking on the phone often," he chimed in.

Marilyn felt sad, but this time around, it wasn't the total devastation she felt when her relationship with Michael ended. Her heart was broken then, and her dream of marrying him was destroyed. She felt herself getting closer and closer to Richard, but she wasn't deeply in love with him, yet. At this time in her life, her career was very important.

Richard was also sad, but it wasn't the heartache of when he lost his wife. He cared deeply for Marilyn, but also at this time in his life, his career opportunity was important.

They enjoyed the rest of the evening, laughing as they always had done, and then called it a night.

Chapter Nineteen
Surprise Meeting

Things were going well for Michael. His hard work paid off in his business and he was very successful. After so many years, he was finally getting into another relationship after his relationship with Marilyn ended mysteriously. He never really understood what had happened. Nothing made sense to him, no matter how he analyzed it.

He flew into Midland frequently, and sometimes strange things happened---like when the rental car attendant called him by another name as if he had known him forever. Then on another occasion, when he took a client to a nice restaurant for dinner, the valet parking attendant said, "Hey, Dean! Good seeing you again. I'll get your Benz right now," as he looked for the key on the board.

"Thanks---but I'm not Dean. I'm Michael Moran from Houston. I guess I just look like Dean," Michael answered laughing.

The valet parker just stared in disbelief, but there was no key for a Benz---the car that matched Michael's number was a Lincoln. *That's strange. He looks exactly like Dean—spittin' image*, the attendant thought as he ran for the car.

 Then something happened that changed Michael's life completely.

On a Saturday, he flew into the airport in Midland and was walking from the plane into the waiting area when two young children ran up to him and grabbed him around the legs. "Uncle Deanie! Uncle Deanie!" they screamed. One was a little girl about four years of age, and the other was a little boy around five or six years of age.

"Hey! Hold on guys! I'm not Uncle Deanie!" Michael called out while searching for the parents of the two children. They either didn't hear him or were so excited that they ignored what he said. They just kept hugging his legs and giggling.

Finally, a father-type came to Michael's rescue. "Hey Dean! Glad to see you. We were just here to pick up Gina's sister and didn't expect to run into you! Glad we did!" the young father said.

"I'm actually not Dean. I'm Michael Moran from Houston. But, a lot of people think I'm Dean," Michael said apologetically.

"You're kidding me, right? Come on, Dean. It hasn't been *that* long since we saw you last!" the man answered jokingly.

"No, I'm being serious," Michael answered. "But, one day it was the valet parking attendant and on another day it was the rental car attendant who thought I was Dean."

"Man, I'm telling you that you are exactly Dean. You look exactly like him. Were you adopted by any chance?" the man inquired.

"Yes, actually I *was* adopted," Michael answered with a puzzled look on his face.

With that answer, the man said, "Would you go with me to the telephone? Dean is a good friend of ours, and he is like an uncle to my children---guess ya could tell that—and I have time before the flight comes in. Let's go call Dean and ask him if he was adopted."

"I'm game," said Michael wondering where all of this was going to lead.

The children couldn't really follow what was happening and wondered why their Uncle Deanie wasn't as warm as friendly as he had always been, so they just stared. Their father explained that Michael wasn't Uncle Deanie. Now, they were really confused. They just kept staring at Michael.

2

Just a few steps down the hallway was a pay phone and the kid's father dialed his friend Dean.

"Hello?" Dean answered.

"You're not gonna believe this, Dean. I am standing here with a guy who looks exactly like

106

you---I mean *exactly*! He even sounds like you. The kids thought he was you! They ran to him, grabbed him around his legs, and started screaming, 'Uncle Deanie!' You've got to see this guy. By the way, were you adopted by your parents?" he managed to ask.

"Interesting, yes, I was adopted," Dean said. The man turned to Michael and nodded.

"What is your birthday?" the kids' father asked.

"April 13, 1952," he answered repeating the date so Michael could hear it. The man turned to Michael who nodded again. It was Michael's birthday, too!

"Oh, my gosh---did you know you had a brother? You never told me that!" the man said excitedly.

"No, I was never told I had a twin. I'm sure my parents were never told," Michael answered.

"We need to get together asap. Dean, can you meet tonight or tomorrow night for dinner or for lunch or something? Michael, can you?" the kids' father said as fast as he could and with a feeling of total excitement.

The three of them agreed on a mutual time to meet on the next evening. How exciting!!!

The kids' father, William, made it to the selected restaurant first. He wanted to make sure he was there to see Michael and Dean when they first saw each other. *This is going to be too good to be true,* he thought.

William got to the restaurant ten minutes before Dean walked through the door. Even then, William told himself to look twice because it just might be Michael instead of Dean. He couldn't tell them apart! "Dean?" William questioned just to make sure.

"No, I'm Michael. Nice seeing you again," Dean said pulling a prank on William. William just stared. Then Dean started laughing and William figured the prank out. "Stop it!" Will said. "I'm having a difficult enough time with the two of you!"

They took a seat near the window so they could see Michael when he arrived at the restaurant. They were both looking out of the window when Michael's car pulled up and Michael got out of the car. "Are you kidding me?" Dean said, "Really?" Dean couldn't believe the man walking up to the door. Dean saw himself walking to the door.

As Michael walked through the door, both Dean and William jumped up to greet him. After a big hug, the twins stared at each other. "I must be looking in a mirror," Michael said. "I'm still in a state of shock."

"Michael, I can't tell you how glad I am that we actually found each other after all of these years. Our next step needs to be to tell our parents. They may be more shocked than we are. Are your parents still living?" Dean asked.

"Yes, my parents are fine. Let's plan how we're gonna tell them. I guess there's an outside chance that they knew we were twins and never said anything, but I don't really think so. They've always been so open about the adoption," Michael offered.

"My parents were always open about my adoption also. I can't see them keeping a secret like that. That's why I think they'll be blown away by this news," Dean said.

William was watching this movie unfold in front of his eyes with a smile on his face. After all, he was the one who ran into Michael at the airport and got this movie started! He had to give credit to his young children who almost tackled Michael there, too. He wondered what his children were gonna think when they see both men together for the first time. He couldn't wait! In fact, everyone who knows Dean will probably freak out when they see the two together! It will be so unexpected.

As the three sat in the restaurant, they went back and forth on the similarities in their lives.

"Are ya married? Do ya have any kids?" Dean asked.

"Nah, I thought I was gonna get married once, but it didn't work out," Michael answered remembering the heartache of losing Marilyn many years ago.

"Yeah, me neither," Dean said. I thought I was gonna get married and it didn't work out either. "So far, our lives were the same." Both guys laughed before continuing the comparison.

"What sports did you play growing up?" Michael asked Dean.

"I played football in middle school and high school, but I also wrestled in high school," Dean responded.

"Oh my gosh---same with me." Michael said. "Hey—what position did you play in football?"

"I played linebacker----you?" Dean answered wondering if their positions would be exactly the same. That would *really* be coincidental!

"Half-back," Michael said, "But, I also played linebacker one time.

"What kind of grades did you make in school?" Dean asked laughing.

"Why are ya laughing? You have trouble? I pretty much was a straight A student," Michael boasted.

"Oh, brother! I struggled the whole time," Dean said looking sad. Then he added, "Nah, not really. I was straight A, also." Now the conversation was getting really interesting. How could they be so *identical*? It's one thing to look *identical* but to have done everything the same way also? Crazy.

"Where did ya go to college?" Michael asked.

"I decided to go to Princeton and was lucky to get accepted," Dean explained. "What about you?"

"I went to Yale and I felt lucky to get accepted, also!" Michael answered the same way.

"What was your major?" Dean asked.

"Finance," Michael answered.

"Economics," Dean said, "Of course."

The guys got such a kick out of finding out that their lives had paralleled in so many ways. William just sat back and listened. It was so interesting.

4

The conversation continued for quite some time before they decided to figure out how to tell their parents. They wanted it to be orchestrated perfectly. "Why don't I fly my parents here telling them I have a surprise for them. You can get your parents to the restaurant. I know one that has a private party room that would be perfect. We won't tell them anything---we'll wait to see how they respond when they see us together," Michael said.

"That's a good idea. Hey---why don't we try to dress alike also---ya know---just to jazz it up a little," Dean offered laughing at the idea.

"Perfect," Michael said. "After the shock of seeing us as twins, we can talk about how this all came about. Then we can ask them if they ever knew anything about twins when they adopted us."

"I'll be shocked if they knew anything," Dean said and Michael agreed. Both men felt that their parents would have told them from the very beginning if that had been the fact.

Other questions popped into their heads and the conversation continued. "Did you ever smoke?" Dean asked.

"Are ya kidding? We were athletes, ya remember? I'd never smoke and I know you were the same---- right?" Michael responded already knowing the answer.

"Right!" Dean said. "No drinking either?"

"Nope---maybe a beer or two on the weekend but no hard liquor," he responded. Michael nodded in agreement. "In fact, never got drunk in my life."

"Now that your football and wrestling days are over, what do you do for a sport?" Michael asked.

"Golf---whenever I can." Dean said.

"Same here----what's your handicap?" Michael asked.

"I'm about an 10----you?" Dean said.

"Of course---about the same," Michael said shaking his head in amazement.

By now the restaurant was getting ready to close for the evening. The men exchanged phone numbers and decided to stay in touch to plan for the twin reveal dinner. They agreed to find old pictures to share when they get together.

Michael and Dean started collecting pictures of
their lives in preparation of sharing them with each
other and with both sets of parents when they meet
for dinner. Both men even asked their parents for
old picture albums without sharing what they
needed them for. Then the day of the "twin reveal"
came. Michael and his parents flew to Midland and
rented nice hotel rooms near the restaurant where
the meeting would take place. Dean picked up his
parents and made sure they were in the party room
before the time for Michael and his parents to
arrive. Both sets of parents were very, very curious
as to why they were asked to save this evening for
something special. They had no idea. They just
knew that their sons had been very secretive about
why their childhood pictures and other family
pictures were requested. They didn't question---
they just trusted their sons.

Dean and his parents arrived at the restaurant. His
mother, Joyce, and his father, Clarence, were seated
near one end of the rectangular table. Dean sat with
his face toward the door. They noticed he
nervously watched the door. He was watching for
something, but they didn't know what.

Michael drove his parents to the restaurant and told
the receptionist they were expected in the private
party room. She walked them to the rear of the

building. Michael's heart was pounding. His parents perceived that he was anxious, but they didn't know why. They would soon find out.

As Michael and his parents reached the door to the private party room, Dean jumped up to welcome them. As previously planned, both Michael and Dean were dressed exactly the same. Both wore cream colored dress slacks with a light blue golf shirt. Both wore shoes to match their slacks. Their hair was combed exactly the same way, but that was the way their hair was usually combed anyway.

Dean's parents, Clarence and Joyce Ridnour, looked at the twins in amazement. At first, they couldn't even speak. They just looked, not believing what they saw.

Michael's parents, Bob and Maureen, were equally in shock. They were speechless. They looked at the boys, then at Dean's parents, then at the boys again---back and forth.

At some point, after the initial shock seemed to wear down just a little, the entire group started laughing.

"Oh, my goodness!" Clarence said, "I guess I know what the big secret is now!"

"This is the most amazin' thing I have ever seen!" Joyce exclaimed. "I never knew you were a twin, Dean, but obviously you are!"

"We didn't know, either," Michael's parents said. That was just what the twins thought---their parents weren't told.

The four people sat down at the table and started going through all of the pictures. They couldn't even think of dinner. They were too excited to see the pictures of the twins as they grew up. Finally, after the waiter made his third appearance, they decided to go ahead and order from the menu. The discussion throughout the meal was very interesting to everyone. Michael and Dean gave a quick review of the things that they had found out about each other the first time they met. That was extremely interesting to the parents.

Then the conversation turned from jovial, light hearted laughter to a little bit of anger.

"When we adopted, we were never told that there was a twin involved. I believe they should have told us. It's just not right to keep that secret from us. The part I hate the most is that these guys should have grown up together. We would have certainly adopted *both* baby boys---no doubt," Michael's parents said.

"Yes, we would have done the same. Absolutely. These boys have missed out on so much that twins usually enjoy," Dean's parents said. "Let's find out why this happened and let's make sure it never happens to anyone else again."

"We may have a little difficulty with that," Bob brought up. "The adoption agency we went through has closed. We may be able to find some of the records, though."

"Well, let's do what we can to find out why this happened, but in the meantime, I want the guys to spend as much time together as they can. They have a lot to catch up on," Clarence added.

The four continued to catch up until the night got very late and the restaurant was getting ready to close. They all hugged each other and vowed to stay in touch. The parents of the twins were determined to get to the bottom of the adoption secret and the twins were determined to spend as much time together as possible. After all, they weren't married, had no children, and could get together quite a bit. What a reunion!

2

Michael, who traveled to Midland pretty often on business found out that he could head up the Midland office----so he moved there.

The twins were inseparable. When they weren't working or traveling for work, they were together. They went to the gym together, went to dinner together, and they enjoyed playing practical jokes on their friends.

When the twins showed up together for the first time at William's house, the little kids couldn't take their eyes off of them. All of a sudden, they had *two* Uncle Deanies! They just didn't know what to make of that. Their father explained, "Kids, you know your friends at school---Marc and Eric? Well, they are twins, aren't they? Dean and Michael are just like they are---they're twins."

The explanation was very good, but it didn't keep the kids from staring at them nonstop. William thought it was more that they didn't know which one was Uncle Deanie and which one wasn't. They couldn't tell the difference.

Where ever the twins went, heads turned. Many people knew Dean, of course, because he grew up there. But, they never saw two of them! It was exciting. The twins often talked about what they would have done in school if they had grown up together.

"Just imagine---going to school, playing sports and even dating. We could trade out positions and no one would even figure it out. If you were great in math and I were great in chemistry, then I could take your tests and you could take mine! Only problem is that we were both great in math and not so hot in chemistry although we still managed to inch out an A," Michael kidded. He knew they would have never done that anyway.

One night when the guys were out to dinner, the topic of dating came up. They talked about how they dated casually in high school and then how they fell in love only to be devastated by the one they loved.

"I was in college and I fell in love with one of the girls that I had dated for almost two years. We talked about getting married many times. We planned where we would live and how many kids we would have and what kind of house we would live in," Dean explained sadly.

"What happened?" Michael asked.

"I met her for dinner one evening at our favorite restaurant. Since we had talked about getting married, but I knew we would wait til after we graduated, I thought I would give her a diamond necklace. It was going to be a 'promise' ring but only it was a necklace. I thought that would be nice until we get officially engaged. She appeared to really love it. I put it around her neck at the restaurant and she kissed me. Everything seemed great but then as time went on, we just grew apart," Dean tried to explain. "That was a long time ago."

"I kind of had the same experience----of course. I fell in love with a girl I met in college, and we were together as much as we could be. We hit it off perfectly. I even went to her house for Thanksgiving and Christmas. We also talked about getting married. To tell you the truth, I was crazy about her," Michael also explained somewhat sadly.

"What happened?" Dean asked.

"I'm not real sure. She went on a day trip with her mother and I really never heard from her after that. She would always call me after a trip, but I never got a call. I tried calling her and talked to her roommate, but she didn't know where she was, either. Finally, I got in contact with her sister who told me that I shouldn't really call anymore. Supposedly, the girl I was in love with had fallen for someone else. It was a shock. I just couldn't understand how that could happen, but I guess it did. I don't think I ever really got over that," Michael explained sadly.

"Do ya think something happened when she was on the trip with her mother? You said she went on a trip out of town, right?" Dean asked.

"I kept thinking about that. It seems it would be hard to be with your mother and then find and fall in love with another man all at the same time and on the same day. That's why it doesn't make sense," Michael figured.

"I agree with you. Something's crazy about that. So, she never called or talked to you? You never questioned her?" Dean asked sincerely.

"No---never talked to her. When I talked to her sister, she made it pretty clear that I should just *not* call. I guess I believed that to be true. Then as time went by, it would have been more and more difficult. I figured she would have called me, if she really cared about me. She didn't call, so I figured she didn't care anymore. Maybe, I should have done all of that differently. Too late now," Michael explained while shaking his head from side to side.

"Where did your girlfriend go on the day trip with her mom?" Dean asked Michael.

"Come to think of it, I think I remember her saying she was coming here----Midland," Michael answered. Then the guys started thinking.

"What year would that have been? Do you remember about when that occurred?" Dean answered.

"Ok, let me think. I was just finishing up my senior year at the university. It was at the end of the semester—so somewhere about late April or May. Yes, I remember. It was about a week before final exams, because I tried to find Marilyn in her classes where she would be having finals. She wasn't there. So, I'd say in was about the first week in May of my senior year." Michael figured out the exact year and told Dean.

"That's interesting. My girlfriend pretty much dumped me that same summer. Another coincidence. They high-fived each other and started laughing. Nothing more came out of that conversation. And nothing would come out of it for many, many years.

Chapter Twenty-One
Their Parents Investigate

When the Morans and the Ridnours had time to think about the situation, they realized that separating the twins at birth was a huge injustice. They communicated many times and came to the same conclusion. They needed to hire an attorney to investigate the situation. The parents didn't want any monetary settlement---money was not their objective; they just wanted to get to the bottom of what had happened. Who made the decision to keep the twins a secret? Why? They had many more questions than answers.

The twins didn't really have an interest in getting the answers to the questions like their parents did. They were glad that they found each other, and they were making the most of it. They were having fun. They even talked about starting a business together; they talked about investing together.

Meanwhile, their parents were on a mission to get answers.

2

Walking into the tall, office building in downtown Houston, the twins' parents caught the elevator to the tenth floor and the office of Attorney Carla Pickrel. Attorney Pickrel was selected to represent both sets of parents in their case to investigate the adoption of their sons so many years earlier. The parents were there to find out information that Attorney Pickrel had discovered.

"Mr. and Mrs. Moran, Mr. and Mrs. Ridnour, I'm so glad you're here today. I think I have some information that you'll find quite interesting. Jump in any time you have a question," Pickrel started. "The adoption agency you both used for the adoption was closed approximately ten years ago. The records for the agency were stored at the university."

"Why were their records stored at the university. What did the university have to do with adoptions?" Bob asked.

"Exactly," Pickrel continued. "Come to find out, there was a large research experiment conducted with the help of the adoption agency. Doctors at the university wanted to research the difference between identical twins raised in different environments. Psychologists and psychiatrists were instrumental in testing and observing the twins."

"Yes, when Michael was about a year old until he was about ten, there were conversations and tests done yearly. We were told it was just research on adopted children. We didn't mind," Bob said.

"Same thing happened to Dean. We were fine with that. What we didn't know was that the doctors were observing and testing, but they were comparing the twins when no one knew there were twins involved. I wonder how many other families had twins and didn't know it!" Clarence chimed in.

Pickrel continued, "Our investigation turned up over sixty couples who adopted one twin and never knew of the other twin. Evidently, all of the records of the testing and the analysis are in closed files that are not open to the public. We have a legal request in action to unseal those files. I have no idea of what we will find, but at least we will get names of the doctors who organized this research. I don't know if any of those people will still be alive, but we will find out. At least we will get some of our questions answered."

The parents thanked attorney Pickrel for her work and agreed to return when additional information was available.

As the couples rode down the elevator and walked out the front of the building, they agreed to have dinner together to discuss everything. Even though they had plenty to talk about concerning the research, instead, they chose to discuss the lives of the boys and how similar things in their lives were---or how similar the boys were.

There were many, many more similarities. Both were in the hospital when young with a bout of pneumonia. Both were in the Boys Scouts and achieved their Eagle Scout Award. Both boys loved the color burgundy. Both boys hated pickles, okra, broccoli, and tuna. How interesting.

Chapter Twenty-Two
Middle Years Fly

Once Michael and Dean found each other, they were determined to catch up on the fun that should have had all along. But now, it might be better than it would have been before. After all, no one knew until the boys told them that they were twins. Their friends never knew they were twins either, so they took that fact a little further.

One day at Dean's office, he and Michael decided to play a joke on the administrative assistant, Shane. Both boys dressed exactly alike. They looked exactly the same. Shane's desk was just across from the conference room. Michael walked past Shane, winking at her like Dean always did, and walked into the conference room. Of course, she thought it was Dean. The door to the conference room closed. Not one minute later, Dean walked up to her desk to hand her something and she looked astonished. She couldn't believe Dean was standing right in front of her when she just saw him walk into the conference room.

"Dean! What? I just saw you walk into the conference room! How can you be here now? I can't believe it!!" Shane said extremely perplexed.

"Oh, that. It's nothing. I took lessons one time from a magician and he taught me how to be in two places at one time. Hey---can ya file this for me? I have to get back to a phone call," Dean said turning and walking down the hall to his office.

Not one minute later, Dean---really Michael--- walked out of the conference room and said, "See?" and he winked at her. Shane just stared not saying a word. 'Dean---really Michael' and his client walked down the opposite hall.

They had barely gotten out of sight when Dean appeared again at her desk. "What did ya think about that?" Dean asked.

"I don't…..I can't…..no way…..how did ya…," Shane was totally confused. Her brain told her that what she *saw* was impossible and there was *no way* Dean could be in two places at one time, but on the other hand, she saw with her own eyes that Dean appeared her and then there and then back again! Shane just shook her head.

Finally, at the end of the day, both Michael and Dean appeared in front of Shane at her desk. "Oh my gosh!" she exclaimed. "Oh my! This is unbelievable! I actually thought I was going crazy! Y'all are *crazy!*"

The guys played that joke on several unsuspecting people until the word got around----and it got around pretty fast.

The last time they tried the identical twin trick, they tried it at Dean's bank. One Saturday, Michael took a check that Dean was going to cash and drove through the drive through banking lane. Since it was a rather large check, the drive through teller had to take it to the manager on duty for approval. The teller had the check and Michael gave her Dean's driver's license. Dean had banked there for many years and all of the bank employees knew him well. At the same time, Dean had walked into the bank lobby and up to the teller window like he had done a million times. Everyone knew him by name. He, too, presented a rather large check to be cashed, so the teller took it to the manager on duty for approval.

The drive through teller had Dean's driver's license and check. The lobby teller had Dean's check and he was standing there at the window. He turned around and waved at the manager like he had done a million times. He knew her personally as well. They had had long conversations together many times in her office. What a puzzle!

"Did you see the person in the car?" the manager asked the drive through teller.

"Yes! Dean is out there in his car. I can see him easily! It's Dean. It's his car. It's his check and his license!" the teller exclaimed.

"But, look whose standing there in our lobby! Isn't that Dean?" the manager asked.

"Uh----uh----yeah---that's Dean. Wait----wait," the drive-through teller answered and then ran out of the office and to the drive through teller window. When she got to the window, there was Dean--- really Michael--- in his car waiting. She could see him clearly. Then she ran back into the lobby. There was Dean standing at the teller window waiting.

By this time, the manager and the lobby teller were walking to the drive-through window. They couldn't believe it, either. *How can this be?* They wondered. All three of the bank employees looked at Dean in the lobby and then looked at who they thought was Dean in the car at the drive-through. They went back and forth. Dean acted like nothing was happening. He just watched the action unfold in front of him. It was all he could do to keep from laughing.

"Dean," the manager finally said to him. "We have a person who looks exactly like you in the drive-through with your license and your check to cash. How is that possible?"

"Oh, well, I needed two checks cashed, so I thought it would be faster to do one in the drive-through and one in the lobby. I don't normally split myself into two people unless I'm in a hurry," he answered nonchalantly.

The girls just stared at him. There was dead silence. Then the guys thought it was time to put the joke to rest. Michael left Dean's car parked in the drive-through and walked into the lobby. When the bank employees saw the two guys together they died laughing.

"Dean! We had no idea you had an identical twin! Why didn't you ever tell us!" the manager said.

"That's because we didn't even know about each other until just recently. We found each other quite by accident, but we've had a good time ever since!" Dean explained.

2

While Michael and Dean were having fun sharing their lives with each other and building new businesses---and playing jokes on people--- Marilyn was enjoying her life, also. She had several hobbies that she really enjoyed. She had been so busy with her educational profession that she had little time for anyone else. Her tutoring kept her so busy, she didn't have time to do all of the things she wanted to spend time on. After thirty years in education, Marilyn decided to retire. She absolutely loved the school district that she had worked in for almost thirty years, but she felt it was time to do other things. She even moved to San Antonio.

After she retired, she continued tutoring and testing students. When she wasn't doing that, she worked in her yard. She absolutely loved building a beautiful back yard. Planting caladium bulbs and then watching them grow was thrilling to her. *I must have a really boring life if watching caladium bulbs come up is exciting to me. Think about it. I go out every morning to see if my caladium bulbs have come up. Oh look! There's one! Wow!* Marilyn thought to herself.

It was exciting to Marilyn to plant all kinds of beautiful plants---many of them tropical. In addition to the lovely, green plants, she found interesting little creatures in her gardens. She had never seen a tiny frog the size of her little fingernail. It was so tiny. A little research on her part told her it was called a Texas Tiny Frog. She was amazed----had never seen one in her whole life so she felt incredibly lucky. *Incredibly lucky to see a little frog? See, that is how exciting my life is*, she thought to herself again.

Then one beautiful, early morning when she went out to water the plants, she saw another unusual creature. Climbing up the side of the house, a shiny-looking, striped lizard with a bright blue tail appeared right before her. Marilyn couldn't believe her eyes. A lizard with a blue tail? She knew she had to research that one for sure. She found out the lizard was called a Blue-Tailed Skink. Creative name. Then she saw a Red-Headed Skink. That's right. It's a lizard with a red head. Creative name.

Marilyn's garden presented her with beautiful birds and unusual frogs. She had unusual lizards, weird spiders, and wild rabbits. She loved all of God's creatures.

In addition to gardening, and particularly in the winter time when she did no gardening, Marilyn loved to crochet. She made afghans to give to her family and friends. Each afghan took approximately fifty hours to complete, so it was a labor of love. Giving afghans to her friends and family members gave her great joy.

Another hobby Marilyn rediscovered after she retired was art. She had always drawn pictures, but she actually took oil painting classes and took to them immediately. She loved painting. Then, one day in her art class, she saw another student using pastels to draw a portrait. Finding that medium fascinating, Marilyn bought the pastel chalks that her teacher suggested and she learned to paint portraits with pastels. Again, she found the hobby very rewarding.

Marilyn's garden was her retreat. After buying her home in San Antonio, she noticed a section of the yard that had been used as a dog run. It was a level below the rest of the yard and was separated by a row of hedges so no one ever saw it, unless they ventured down several stone steps to the lower level. The area was long and relatively narrow. Marilyn could envision a checkerboard pattern of square concrete blocks set diagonally and separated by three-inch sections of green synthetic turf.

When it was time for the turf to be cut and laid down, a nice friend came over and the two of them used scissors to cut the turf. It took hours! They were sitting on the concrete pool decking to do it. A small board was used to make the cuts straight and evenly spaced. Gloves tried to protect their hands from blisters, but that only lasted a short time. She thought it would only take a little time and not cost much at all. In ended up taking a lot of time and it cost quite a bit! But, it was worth it in the end. The project looked absolutely beautiful. I large urn on a pillar on the far end of the yard past the diagonal squares held a large fern that draped gracefully over the side of the urn to the pillar. On each side of the pillar stood two graceful angel statues. They were over five feet tall. How picturesque! So, with that, Marilyn named her little garden area the Secret Angel Garden. Additional angels were added along either side.

When Marilyn found garden stakes that could be written on in her favorite gardening catalogue, she purchased some to write the names of friends and family who had passed away. It became a memorial for those close to her. An angel kneeling down in prayer looked over the names.

Over time, the angel garden expanded to include the upper garden area. She needed more room for the angels she collected or were given. On at least two occasions, she bought an angel or was given an angel that seemed just too perfect to put out in the yard and weather. Those angels were placed inside where Marilyn enjoyed them each and every day. One particular angel that she cherishes is a cream-colored angel about twelve inches tall given to her from her best friend. It is very detailed and a true work of art.

Although Marilyn never married, and still had feelings of sorrow if she allowed her mind to wander back to her college days when she was in love with Michael, she found a way to find comfort in her work and her hobbies. She was happy and was content. Then something happened to turn her life around once again.

Chapter Twenty-Three
Puzzle Probably Solved

Michael and Dean were busy entrepreneurs; their adventures created a large amount of wealth for both of them. The relationship that Michael thought might work out with Stella didn't actually work out. That just left more time for the twins to be together. They enjoyed working and playing. One evening over dinner, the conversation once again turned to the women in their lives----- who left them.

For Dean, it was the college sweetheart who accepted his diamond necklace as a "promise" necklace in preparation for becoming engaged after graduation. They grew apart. For Michael, it was Marilyn who went on a day trip with her mother and then never talked to Michael after that. When he reached out, Marilyn's sister told him she had found someone else and it would be better not to call her again. So, he didn't. For years after that, he wished that he had gotten some answers, but he just never did.

On one cold, snowy evening, while drinking a beer in front of the crackling logs in Michael's fireplace, Dean had a thought. "Michael, you mentioned that Marilyn had been on a trip with her mother and you think you remember it was to here----to Midland," Dean said.

"Yeah, that was a long time ago, but I think that's where she said she was going with her mom. So, what are ya thinkin'?" Michael questioned.

"You always thought that she had found someone else, because you were goin' by what her sister told you, right?" Dean asked.

"Yep—that's what I've always believed. What else?" Michael asked.

"You said it happened around the end of the second semester of your senior year. Didn't ya?"

"Yeah, must have been late April or May sometime, based on my trying to find her in class during finals week," Michael answered.

"That would have been the *exact* same time I was with my girlfriend all the time. We went to games, went out to dinner, went shopping----you name it. What if Marilyn saw us together and thought it was *you* instead of *me*. That would have been the reason she never called you again. It doesn't make sense that she could find someone else in one day while on a trip with her mom. You should try to check that out," Dean explained.

Michael listened intently with a slight frown on his face. "Ya know? I think you may have figured it all out. If true, that's the saddest thing that could have ever happened. If I had persisted in seeing her, and if I had ignored what her sister told me, I

136

might have found out what happened. If she had told me that she saw me with someone else, I would have had at least a chance of explaining it to her."

"The only problem would be that we looked *exactly* alike in those days----I mean exactly! You've compared our pictures!" Dean said. "She might not have believed you since she saw you----me----with her own eyes."

"Yeah, and her mother was there, also. She would have probably seen you, too," Michael explained.

"That's another problem with the adoption agency not notifying our parents that we were twins. Freak things just like this could happen," Dean said.

"Well, I'd love to know for sure, but it's been so many years. I know that Marilyn is probably married with kids, and I don't want to interrupt her life---not that it would disrupt her life---but I just don't want to bother her," Michael explained reluctantly.

"I understand----it's in the past---leave it alone," Dean added.

Michael couldn't get that thought out of his mind. He kept replaying the scenario over and over in his mind. The more he thought about it, the more it disturbed him. He was concerned about how Marilyn felt if, in fact, she did see Dean with his girlfriend. She must have been extremely hurt, and her mother must have been extremely angry. Michael could imagine Marilyn crying herself to sleep at night, because they were very much in love and were planning for a wedding. Somehow, he'd have to find her and make it right. He was on a mission.

2

Michael went to the house that he remembered Marilyn's parents lived in. They were no longer there. None of the telephone numbers worked either. Finally, he thought the best way to track Marilyn down was to hire a private investigator.

Within a few months, Noah, the private investigator had some information for Michael.

"Michael, Marilyn is now living in San Antonio. She retired from public school education but continues to do a great deal of volunteer work and some tutoring. She never married..." Noah continued until Michael interrupted.

"She never married?" Michael asked.

"No, she never married. There are no records of a marriage," Noah said.

"Do you have her current address and telephone number?" Michael asked.

"Am I a private investigator?" Noah teased.

"Ok---of course, you have all that information. I just can't believe she never married," Michael said with a stunned look on his face. "I'll see if I can talk to her and visit with her. We have a lot to catch up on."

Chapter Twenty-Four
The Reunion

Michael thought about the information he had received from the investigator. He wanted to talk to Marilyn and find out if she had, in fact, mistaken Dean for him those many, many years ago. He wondered if any particular incident had caused the problem that caused their breakup. Even if Marilyn were very happy in her current life, he wanted to set the past straight. He needed to get that message to her.

He thought and thought about the best way to meet Marilyn. *Should I write a letter? That would give her a way out if she didn't want to ever see me again. She could just opt to not call me. I'll give her that option. Should I just appear at her door? That might be too awkward and too much of a surprise. Also, if she is spending her life with someone, that could be very awkward----your old boyfriend showing up on your front porch! No, I won't do that. I could call, but that might be awkward also. It would be a surprise for sure, and the timing might not be right. No, I think I will write the letter and leave it up to her. She'll have time to process my request and make a decision in her own time.*

Michael started the letter:

Dear Marilyn,

I know this letter may come as somewhat of a surprise to you, but I think it is important that we discuss an incident that happened many years ago. There is reason to believe that the whole thing was a serious case of miscommunication. I would never have understood why we possibly broke up our relationship had it not been for an accidental discovery. I found out quite by accident that I have an identical twin. I have pictures of my twin at about that same time and he looks exactly the way I did. We wore our hair the same, we were the same height and weight, and our mannerisms were the same. I don't know if you will be interested, but I would like to talk to you about what happened the end of my senior year in college which would have been the end of your sophomore year, right before finals. If you are not interested, or if your life is too busy, I will understand. I just wanted to clear something up that has been bothering me all of my life. My telephone number is 214-554-0385.

Fondly,
Michael

Michael popped the letter in the mail and waited.

2

Marilyn was enjoying a morning walk in the neighborhood and around the lake on the morning that the letter reached her mailbox. She always enjoyed seeing the ducks swimming in the lake and loved the cool breeze as it swirled through the trees in the park. She often thought to herself how lucky she was to live in such a pretty environment.

On this particular morning, she stopped by her mailbox to retrieve her mail, before she went inside the house. Glancing through the junk mail and tossing the weekly advertisements, she caught a glance of the envelope with the name 'Michael Moran' in the left-hand corner. *That can't be the Michael I used to know*, she thought. *This is probably junk mail, too.* But she tossed it on her desk while she went around to sit in the desk chair.

Sliding the letter opener along the edge to open the envelope, she pulled out the letter and opened it. She read it aloud hesitantly.

"Dear Marilyn,…….I know this letter may……" then she read silently the rest of the way very puzzled at what she read. *Is this real? Did something like this really happen?* Her brain was a whirr. She remembered the incident vividly. It had replayed in her mind a million times over the years. Even when she wanted to forget it, she couldn't. It was like a video that was permanently fixed in her mind. The video was always the same. Marilyn and her mother were in the restaurant during a day trip to Midland. Once they were seated, she noticed the person she thought was Michael in a booth not too far back from her. He was with a young, beautiful girl and appeared to be infatuated with her. At one point, he gave the girl a necklace and she kissed him. They held hands across the table. It was Michael. Even Marilyn's mother noticed and confirmed it was Michael. But now, Michael is saying that it was probably his identical twin. After all of these years, no one would go to that much trouble to make up a story or to even follow up with it unless it were true. Marilyn decided she needed to talk to Michael to find out for sure. *This is going to be very interesting*, she thought.

3

Marilyn paced the room a few times deciding what she would say on the phone. Then she placed the phone call:

"Hello?" Michael answered not knowing who was on the other end of the line.

"Michael? This is Marilyn. I got your letter and you were right---I was *very* surprised!" she said cheerfully. "It's been a long time—how are ya doin'?"

"Oh, I'm fine, Marilyn. I just wanted to talk to you to catch you up on what I found out about my life since we broke up those many years ago. It's quite interesting to say the least. I'm happy to talk on the phone, but I was hoping you'd have time to go to dinner some evening. I think this could take a while," he asked hoping she would agree to dinner. "Or take you and your significant other if you have one." Michael had been told by the investigator that Marilyn wasn't married, but he didn't know if there was someone else in the picture.

"Sure, sounds good to me---no, no one else," she answered cheerfully. "Are you gonna be in San Antonio which also brings me to the question--- How did you find me?"

"It wasn't easy finding you, but I'll explain all that when we meet. Yes, I'll be in San Antonio this weekend. Does that work for you?" he asked.

"Yes, I don't have any commitments for this weekend. I'm pretty free, so you tell me," she answered already feeling the excitement in her heart. *Don't get excited,* Marilyn told herself. *He's probably married with five kids and four grandchildren.*

"Ok, I'll pick out a good restaurant, and I'll pick you up at 6:30 pm sharp. We have a lot of catching up to do," he answered.

"Do you know where I live?" Marilyn asked sincerely.

"Marilyn, yes, I know where you live. Remember, I found you." They laughed that same familiar laugh they had together when they were still young. Marilyn decided not to mention anything to her mother until she heard the whole story. Her mother had also been in on the situation those many years ago, too.

4

Saturday was a great day. The sun shone brightly, but it wasn't hot. It was still early Spring and although the plants and flowers were starting to look quite beautiful, the sun had not commanded its presence in the form of intense heat, yet. Michael had always loved San Antonio. It was a large town that just seemed small and friendly. He had done business there over the years, never knowing that Marilyn lived there, also.

Michael caught a plane to San Antonio the morning of the day he was to meet Marilyn for dinner. He checked into a hotel and had time to relax before showering and dressing for dinner. He didn't want to allow himself to get excited, because he rationalized that Marilyn *had* to be in another relationship of some sort. He was the one free and clear of any relationships. He had accepted his life as a bachelor and had actually enjoyed it for the most part. The same was true of his twin brother, Dean. Dean never married either, so the two of them became the family unit. They had a lot of catching up to do also, having missed so many years together. They truly enjoyed the last twenty years that they had been together.

When Michael pulled up to Marilyn's house, he noticed how neatly manicured her front lawn was. He made a note to ask her about her gardener. He had friends there who could always use a great gardener. He noticed the shrubs and the flowers, artistically placed to accentuate the beautiful lines of her home. It was more artistry than gardening and he would mention that to her if he remembered.

Marilyn didn't want to act too anxious, but she had been waiting for him, sitting in her living room----looking out the window for a car. As he walked up the sidewalk, she opened the front door.

"Hey, Michael! You found my house!" she said cheerfully.

"Of course, I did. Who do you think I am, anyway!" he answered as he handed her a long stem pink rose." Michael handed Marilyn the rose and it sent an excited feeling through her body. Michael felt an element of electricity, too. *Isn't this exactly how I used to feel? I wonder if she feels the same way.* Marilyn felt the same way.

"If you're ready to go, let's go!" Michael said. "Do you need your purse or wrap or anything?"

"Let me just run in a minute to get my purse," she said as she walked through the door into the living room. Michael stood on the front porch waiting. Marilyn ran in, retrieved her purse and then shut the door behind her. The two walked to the rental car and Michael helped her in.

The car ride to the restaurant was filled with a million questions, but they decided to wait to sit down to dinner to go over everything in detail. One detail Marilyn found out on the way was that Michael had never married and was not in a relationship of any kind now. Michael told her he had several pictures that he wanted to show her; the only thing that Marilyn brought was a small sack of M&M's that she hid in her purse.

5

"Mr. Moran, how nice to see you this evening," the doorman at the restaurant said recognizing him. Walking in, Michael and Marilyn were seated near the back of the restaurant in a very private booth. They stared at each other like they couldn't believe what was happening. It was pretty unbelievable.

"Before I explain what brought us together tonight, let me show you some old photos I brought," Michael said as he pulled several photos from an envelope to show her. "Who is this?" Michael showed her a picture of Dean.

"That's you, Michael. That was right at the time we were together," she answered confidently.

"And this one?" Michael showed her a picture of himself.

"That's you also. Why are you asking me that?" Marilyn answered wondering where he was going with his questioning. She remembered the twin thing, but she didn't think anyone could look that much alike. These pictures had to be Michael.

"Marilyn, like I said in the letter and over the phone, we were very close while we were in college and we were talking about and making plans to get married. Then something strange happened and we were never together again. I never really understood that, but your sister told me you had found someone else, so I backed off. I have kicked myself a million times since then. I should have followed up to make sure. I tried to find you at the university during finals, but you weren't there. Your roommate couldn't tell me anything, either. I finally gave up thinking that you had, indeed, found someone else. I rationalized that you would have called me, unless you had met someone new.

Years later, many years later, a freak incident occurred. I got off an airplane in Midland and was almost tackled by two little kids who yelled, "Uncle Deanie! Uncle Deanie!" I knew I wasn't Uncle Deanie, but I didn't quite know what to do. Fortunately, their father came to my rescue. He thought I was Uncle Deanie, too! I had to convince him that I wasn't. It was at that moment that he figured out I was the twin to one of his best friends, Dean. He called him to ask him if he were adopted and what his birthdate was. I was listening to the conversation. Yep—same birthday. Our parents---both sets---confirmed that they were never told we were twins, so it was just as much of a shock to them. We took months catching up on each other's life. It wasn't until years later that we compared our lives concerning the topic of girlfriends. I don't know why that never came up before. Dean was the one who figured out that he was in Midland when you and your mother were there and he had a girlfriend that he really cared about. He thinks you could have seen them together while you were there---thinking you saw me instead. What do you remember about that trip?" Marilyn could tell that Michael was very serious and was also very concerned about what had happened many years ago. She looked into his eyes and with complete seriousness recollected the event.

"Ok, I remember that my mother asked me to go on a day trip with her to Midland. On the drive there, we had plenty of time to talk about our relationship----yours and mine. Since you and I had talked about getting married, I thought the trip would be the perfect time to discuss it with Mom. She thought so highly of you, that she was perfectly fine with us getting married. I told her we were going to wait until you graduated and found a job and then we would decide on the date and to what university I would transfer. She thought it was a good plan. We finished the work Mom had to do then found a good restaurant to have dinner. We

149

walked in, was seated in a booth, and then I noticed you---or who I thought was you----in a booth behind us over my left shoulder. I noticed you were with a very pretty girl and the two of you were holding hands over the table. So many things were going through my head. First, I couldn't believe you didn't see us walk in. It would almost have been impossible to not see us be seated. The restaurant was pretty small. Then I thought maybe you were with a client, but ya'll seemed a little too familiar with each other for that. And clients don't usually hold hands! Then I saw that you handed her a small box that she opened. She took out a necklace and I could hear her squealing with excitement. You stood up, helped her put it around her neck and them the two of you kissed. My heart sank. I had never felt so low in all of my life. My mother saw it, too. I couldn't even speak. Mom just said, "Come on, let's get out of here." We walked out the door. Evidently you didn't see us leave either. I never looked back, but later, my mother said she turned to look back at you. She said you looked at her with no expression on your face. I never knew that you talked to my sister. It sounds like something she would do, however. I just fell into a deep state of depression and stayed in a dark hole for quite some time. I saw you with that girl and it was *you*-----or so I thought," Marilyn said seriously but without the pain that she felt so many years ago. "Are you telling me you have an *identical* twin? Is that what these pictures are about?"

"Yes, Marilyn, this is *my* picture and this one is *Dean*," Michael said handing her the pictures. She was silent. One could tell questions were swirling in her head. She couldn't believe both pictures were not Michael.

"I can't believe this! I absolutely cannot tell the two of you apart. Same eyes, same hair, same face, same body build, same everything---- everything. I'm in shock."

"Yes-----Marilyn, do you mind if we call Dean right now? He knows I'm having dinner with you and I told him we might have some questions," Michael asked seriously.

"Sure!" she answered getting more excited by the minute.

Michael called Dean and the phone rang only once. "Hey Dean, I'm here with Marilyn who is as beautiful as she was as a sophomore at the university---hasn't changed one bit. Anyway, did you give your girlfriend a necklace in a restaurant?" Michael asked.

"Sure did. Don't ya remember me telling you about that? We were talking about being dumped. I told you I had a girlfriend I was crazy about and wanted to give her a necklace as sort of a 'promise ring' idea. She really loved it. She loved *it*, but she didn't love *me*!" They both laughed at that one. "But, yeah, it was in a restaurant in Midland." Marilyn could hear the conversation.

"OK---stay tuned," Michael said and he hung up the phone.

"Oh, Michael…oh, Michael…..," tears started streaming down her cheeks. "How could something like that happen to us? Why? I'm devastated. The pain I went through---and I guess you did, too----for nothing."

"Marilyn, we'll never know, and we'll never understand why things happened the way they did. We can never go back. We can, however, go forward," Michael said as he brushed a tear off her cheek with his finger. "I love you, Marilyn. I have always loved you. Seeing you now is no different from seeing you back in our college days."

Marilyn looked into his eyes and she felt the same way. *How can so many years go by and it feel like minutes?* she thought to herself. She reached into her purse and pulled out the small bag of M&Ms . She handed him the bag. Michael looked into her eyes and he teared up, too. *Oh my gosh*, he thought.

"I'll never, ever forget all the M&M pranks we played on each other. I've thought about them hundreds of times over the years. Every time I think of them, I smile. Now you beat me at our old game, again----but barely." Michael then pulled a small bag of M&M's out of his jacket pocket. Marilyn threw her arms around him and they held each other in their arms. The love they had for each other had never left. It just lay dormant for many, many years, but maybe to come back stronger than ever.

"I've got to meet Dean. I've got to tell my mother. I've got to tell my sister. I have a hundred things swirling through my head right now!" she said excitedly.

"We have so much catching up to do! You can't believe what happened when Dean and I introduced ourselves to both sets of parents one evening. Our parents were never told when they adopted us that we were identical twins. As far as they knew, they were adopting a single baby boy. At first, they were amazed but then that amazement turned into anger. They were angry because they felt that we should have been together growing up. Both sets of parents told us that they would have gladly adopted *both* baby boys," Michael explained.

"Why did the adoption agency keep it a secret?" Marilyn asked sincerely. "I don't see the purpose."

"It was actually an experiment; we were research topics studied through the university attached to the hospital. Our parents hired attorneys who are looking into other families who raised twins separately from the same adoption agency.

Dean and I don't care. I mean, we *do* care, because we don't want other twins to miss out on finding each other, but we're just glad *we* found each other. Our lives have been so busy trying to catch up on the time we've missed-----and now here *you* are!"

"Now here *I* am? Sounds like drudgery to me," she commented kiddingly as she took his hand in hers.

"Are ya kidding? Finding you again is one of the best things that could possibly happen to me. First, finding my brother----then finding you. The questions I have had throughout my life have been answered. I'm at peace for the first time since the age of twenty," Michael explained leaning over to kiss Marilyn on the cheek.

"I've had a good life. It's not the life I would have had if we had been together, but after the severe depression, I pulled myself out of a hole and started living again. I poured myself into my profession and became—what I thought---was successful. I was actually felt happy and fulfilled. I met several people along the way and had good relationships, but nothing ever developed into anything serious. How about you?" Marilyn asked.

"Kind of the same here. I was devastated when we split up, so I poured myself into my job. I worked many, many hours every day and all weekend. I wasn't interested in dating, because I was working all the time. I felt driven to become as

154

successful as I could be, as fast as I could be. I dated a few girls later, but very casually---nothing serious. Then Dean came into my life and it became a whirlwind. We started working and investing together and had no time for anyone else, really. We felt we had to catch up on all the years we missed knowing each other. We have, truthfully, had a blast. But, now, I want you in my life also. You're not in a relationship now?"

Marilyn smiled then answered, "No, I met a really nice man and we enjoyed being together, but it just wasn't meant to be. In fact, he has moved to another state to pursue a great job."

"Ya didn't want to go with him?" Michael asked hoping she'd answer the way he wanted her to.

"No, I have my life here. I think the world of him, but it's not serious. We're great friends. We can talk on the phone," she answered.

Michael felt good about their conversation; he didn't want the night to end. He knew sitting there looking into Marilyn's eyes that they would be together for the rest of their lives. He had no doubt. Marilyn felt the same way. They would pick up right where they left off those many, many years ago. Only this time, they would have other family members to spend time with. Dean was an integral part of the family as Michael was with his family. Their lives and businesses had become intertwined.

With the addition of Marilyn, everyone's life was enhanced.

6

Michael told his parents everything that had happened with Marilyn. They had never understood the situation either, other than probably Marilyn had met someone else many years ago. They never mentioned her name, knowing how hurtful it was to Michael. They had been shocked at finding out about Michael's twin but never put that together with the split up earlier, either. Too many years had passed. When Michael told them the story, they were in awe. Then when Michael told him that he and Marilyn and reconnected, they were ecstatic. They wanted him to be with someone special to spend his life with and Marilyn certainly fit that criteria.

Then Marilyn took Michael to her parents' home to tell them about the discovery. She told them ahead of time that he'd be coming with her. Her parents were quite curious about the whole thing.

"Mom, Dad----I'm sure you remember Michael. The last time we were together was when I was finishing my sophomore year in college and he was completing his senior year," she started then continued, "We were talking about getting married and then something terrible happened. Remember, Mom? You and I were on that day trip to Midland? Remember we were in the restaurant and we saw

156

Michael with a pretty girl? Remember he gave her a necklace and they kissed?"

"Yes," Mrs. Johnson responded. "I remember vividly as if it were yesterday. And what I remember most was how we lost our little girl to depression that lasted for several months."

"I know, Mom. I know. Well, you're not gonna believe this probably, but that wasn't Michael. It was Dean----his identical twin. Michael never even knew he had an identical twin until many, many years later. His parents didn't know either. Dean's parents didn't know, either. But, it's true. Look at these pictures----this is Dean----this is Michael around that same time. Here---here are some more pictures of them growing up."

"No one would believe this story," Mr. Johnson said shaking his head. "Is this really true?" he asked Michael.

"Mr. Johnson, I promise you, this is the truth. I know it sounds like something you'd see in a movie, but it really happened that way. I didn't even know about the restaurant thing 'til Dean and I had been together several years. The conversation somehow turned to girlfriends dumping us and that's how it came up. But, I swear, it is the truth," Michael answered with complete conviction.

Marilyn's parents believed him. They felt his truthfulness. "So, you thought Marilyn had dumped you, and she thought you had dumped her?" her father asked.

"Yes, going back over our memories, we figured out that after Marilyn saw "me" in that restaurant with that girl, she surmised that I wasn't serious about our relationship, and she backed off totally. She disappeared instead of confronting me. She knew what she had seen and Mrs. Johnson, you knew what you had seen also."

"I sure did. As we walked out of the restaurant, I turned around to look at you one last time, and our eyes connected. You didn't even flinch. But now I know why! You didn't even know who we were! You'd never seen us before! Well---I saw 'you' but it must have really been Dean!" Mrs. Johnson answered actually relieved even after all of these years that it really wasn't Michael.

"Believe me---if I could turn back the hands of time, I would. I wouldn't have let Marilyn slip out of my life like I did. But, I was young and foolish, too. When I talked to Marilyn's sister, she told me Marilyn had found someone else and that I shouldn't call her again. And then I figured if it weren't true she would certainly call me----and she never did. Why did this have to happen to us?" Michael said sadly. "I loved Marilyn more than anything else in the whole world and I still do."

Marilyn's parents believed every word Michael and Marilyn told them. They saw how the two looked at each other and how deeply in love they still were. "I have to admit we weren't too fond of you after the incident," Mr. Johnson added. "But that's in the past. I see a very happy future. I'm concerned now that Marilyn's sister is going to take the blame for keeping you two apart. Let's be careful with her."

The foursome talked for several hours before calling it an evening. Then Michael and Marilyn left holding hands while they walked down the sidewalk to the car. They couldn't be happier together.

Chapter Twenty-Five
Their New Life

The trees were full of leaves and flowers were everywhere. Beautiful, fluffy white clouds filled the sky against a vivid-blue sky; butterflies and colorful birds flew around playfully. The world was just a more beautiful place for Marilyn and Michael.

They met with Marilyn's sister Brenda and explained the whole story. They handled it well enough that she didn't feel like it was totally her fault. She did feel, however, that her comment to Michael was instrumental to some extent.

"I'm so sorry----I had no idea. I just remember my baby sister was hurting so much. I couldn't bear to see her in so much pain. We all believed what Mom and Marilyn saw and if that were the case, she didn't need to even be around you, Michael. I'm so sorry," Brenda said almost crying.

"You had no idea. None of us had any idea! It was just a strange coincidence that no one can explain. Don't beat yourself up. I've analyzed this a million times and I blame myself each and every time. Let's not look backward----let's look forward," Michael explained. They all hugged and vowed to follow his advice.

Marilyn and Michael had the time of their lives. They were both retired, so they had plenty of time to travel and visit old friends and relatives. Of course, Dean was an integral part of their lives and he went with them everywhere. The threesome enjoyed each other's company and there was always plenty of laughter.

One evening, after watching a movie on angels, Marilyn commented, "Michael, speaking of angels-----I have to tell you of two different times that an angel---or spirit---or something intervened in my life to protect me."

"Really? Tell me about it," he asked.

Marilyn began, "My friend and I were invited to spend vacation time with some friends who live in the North but have a beautiful home in Cabo San Lucas, Mexico. While they took my friend golfing every day, I stayed in the house overlooking the ocean, relishing the time I had to work on my first novel. I had started it years earlier but never found the time to donate to writing in order to finish it.

On the first night there, we were sitting out on the patio watching the beautiful sunset over the ocean. The sun disappeared and darkness slowly came upon us. I needed to go to the restroom so I opened the sliding glass door to enter the house. No lights were left on, since it was fully light when we went out on the patio. I felt of the wall to locate a light switch but couldn't find it. I knew where the bathroom was, so I made my way there successfully and switched on the light. On the way to the bathroom, I had to take two steps up to the entrance level. Leaving the restroom, I turned off the light and walked toward the wall of windows leading to the patio. Lights from the surrounding houses barely lit up the room, so I walked toward the light cautiously. I totally forgot about the two steps between the entrance level that the restroom was on and the lower level leading to the patio. There was one step between the two levels. As I cautiously walked in the near darkness, I felt the very slightest change in footing but thought nothing of it at the time. I just thought, *"Oh, yes. I forgot about the steps."* I walked through the sliding door and out to the patio where everyone else was talking.

We had a wonderful time on our vacation and after a few days returned to Houston. It wasn't until about two weeks had passed that I started thinking about that night when I walked into the house in the dark. I don't know why that idea popped into my head. I started thinking that there was no way I could have made my way down those two steps in the dark. I had forgotten the steps were there, so I blindly walked past them. How did I not fall? It would basically be impossible to NOT fall. I found an area in my home back in Houston that had a similar step between levels. I pretended that I stepped with my left foot as far on the upper step as possible without feeling my toe going over the edge. Then I took another step forward with my right foot to see if the step on the lower level would work without hitting the middle step with my foot, thus causing a fall. It wasn't possible. I would have had to take a giant step forward to negotiate to the lower level and I know I did not do that. I couldn't do that. I didn't even consider it, since I was walking cautiously forward in the dark. Then I tried it with the opposite foot. I came to the same conclusion. I didn't see any way I could have negotiated that step without falling down. Even a two-inch drop can cause a person to lose his footing and fall. How could it be possible to negotiate a two-step drop without falling? I told myself that maybe the steps in Cabo were possibly more narrow? Possibly shorter? I told myself to check it out, if I were ever in the house again. Then about a year later I had my chance.

About a year later, I was invited to join Pat and Patty again in their home in Cabo. I instantly remembered about the steps. I looked at them when we entered the home. They certainly looked like what I remembered, but I would experiment with them later when no one was around.

The next morning, Joey, Pat and Patty decided to play golf----that was the intent of the whole vacation anyway. That allowed me the quietness to investigate the steps. I did the same experiment I had done in our home in Houston. I placed my left foot as far on the upper step as would be possible. Then I imagined stepping forward unknowing that a step was below. In a normal stride, my right foot hit the edge of the step in the middle of the levels---or would have hit the middle of the step causing a fall. The only way to accomplish a normal stride would have resulted in a bad fall. Changing feet resulted in the same conclusion. The steps were the same and the height was the same so more than likely the steps were considered standard size and depth. How did I not fall? How did I not feel a significant jar! How did I really not feel anything? And why didn't I realize at the time that what I experienced was highly unusual?

I revisited the idea several more times while we were there. I was as puzzled as before. I never mentioned a word of it to anyone. I still needed time to process it myself in my mind. The very least that should have happened if I had actually missed the steps but didn't fall down would have been to feel quite a jar when my foot landed. I felt practically nothing. Certainly not a significant jar!

I remember accidentally missing a step as I came down on a ladder. It as a short ladder with only about three steps. I was decorating the Christmas tree. When my foot reached the first step on the way down, I thought it was the floor level. By being off one step, I twisted my ankle badly and was in pain for weeks. By missing one step, it threw me off completely. That is what made me think so hard about missing two steps completely.

The only explanation that I could possibly come up with for being spared the accident in Cabo was that there was a guardian angel or a guardian spirit that stepped in and rescued me from a terrible fall. The fall could have resulted in broken bones and a spoiled vacation or at least bruising and much pain.

Then another incident occurred several months after our second visit, but this time it occurred in my garden. I love gardening and had been puttering around in the backyard. My friend's wedding had been the day before in the garden. Under one of the wedding cakes was a three-inch slice of a log that acted as a decorative plate for the cake. Since they did not take the log plate with them, I surmised that they did not want it. I saw it as a perfect stand for the small concrete angel sitting on the edge of the rock wall leading to the garden below.

Since the angel was solid concrete and almost three feet tall, it was far too heavy for one person to lift. My friend and I struggled to lift it onto the log stand. Then a call came from the bride, Carla: "Marilyn, do you still have that log slice that was under the wedding cake? If we don't return it, the bakery will charge us $100!"

I explained that, yes, I had what she needed. What I didn't tell her was that we had placed a heavy concrete angel on top of it. It would be OK though. All I needed to do was move the angel, get the piece of wood, and wipe off any dirt that may have gotten on it. No problem.

I knew I should have waited for help, but I wasn't for sure when the bride was going to come by to retrieve the piece. I also knew there was no way to lift the angel on my own, but I thought about the physics problem concerning fulcrums and leverage. If I tilted the angel at just the right angle, the weight of the angel would fall on the corner and all of the weight would be pushing down there, similar to using a dolly and getting the load at the right angle where the load on the wheels is not heavy. When the angle is right, a large and very heavy refrigerator can be moved fairly easily.

I thought if I reached my arm around the concrete angel, I could tilt her at just the right angle and then slowly inch her over to the edge of the wood piece. At the edge of the wood, she would drop down approximately three inches to the top of the stone wall. It would work, I thought. Even if she fell over because I didn't have the angle right, she would not be damaged. Either way, she would be off the wood piece and I could get it ready for the bride to pick up.

I knelt down, put my arm around the angel, and began inching her to the edge of the piece of wood. It wasn't that difficult since she was at an angle. I kind of walked her to the edge. Just as I tried to drop her off the edge of the wood onto the wall three inches below, I felt her weight shift. I had miscalculated. She was falling and there was no way I could stop her. I felt my body falling to the left. The only thing to my left was a large boxwood shrub. I knew there was no way to recover from my fall. I was falling and I couldn't stop it. Then out of nowhere, I bounced up and was even able to put the angel back where she had been sitting. In my mind, all I remember thinking was, *"Wow, that shrub was really flexible. It pushed me right up when I was falling and was totally off balance."* I was actually amazed that the boxwood was that flexible.

It was not until two weeks later that I was again working in the backyard and a thought popped into my head. Did that really happen to me? Did I fall and get pushed back up by a shrub? I walked over to the angel, knelt down, and pretended I was falling into the boxwood shrub to my left. There was no flexibility. There was no bounce. When I pushed on the bush, it pushed in----it didn't bounce back. If I had fallen into the shrub, that is where I would have ended up. In addition, I distinctly remembered a push from the back left. Kneeling down, the only thing to the back and to the left, was a very large pot. For sure, that pot did not push me back up.

I revisited that scenario over and over. I revisited the feeling I had while I was falling. I was going down---no way to recover. I remembered the push from the back and left but thinking it was the shrub. I remember being pushed right back up and, in addition, being able to push the concrete angel back upright. That in itself would have been impossible also, but I didn't think about it at the time. I didn't tell anyone for at least three months. I needed time to analyze the incident completely.

I noticed a pattern. After the incident in Cabo with the steps, and after this incident with the concrete angel, I thought nothing of what happened, or thought little of what had happened at the time. It was only days later that I started thinking and the questions started coming. There were two times when unbelievable things happened to me, yet at the time, I didn't see them as unbelievable! In the case of the concrete angel, I was so amazed that the shrub pushed me up that I didn't realize it was impossible. I didn't even think about the fact that I missed two steps because I was just trying to reach the sliding door.

I have gone over those incidents many, many times. I have tried to analyze them from a scientific point of view. I have tried to analyze them on a purely coincidental point of view. I have come up with only one conclusion----I have a guardian angel who has stepped in two times to save me from danger or to help me. I challenge anyone else to come up with another explanation. I welcome your opinion. It could be that other things have happened in my life with some form of angel intervention, but I never recognized them as such. Did my guardian angel prevent me from a terrible accident in Cabo? Did my guardian angel prevent an accident with my concrete angel? I have no way of knowing, but I have a way of believing. I believe in angels."

"That's pretty amazing," Michael responded after listening to the entire story. "I'd have no other answer on how that could possibly happen."

"I wish someone could explain it to me in any other way other than an angel. Maybe I should just accept it. Maybe I should be ecstatic I had an encounter with an angel. When I think about it, I actually am ecstatic," Marilyn answered.

3

Since Michael found Marilyn, they had not spent at least part of everyday together. He moved to San Antonio and rented a small house really close to where Marilyn's house was located. They considered moving in together but decided to give their relationship time to adapt to their new lives.

Marilyn had her flower gardens where she spent her early mornings and Michael had his vegetable gardens where he puttered around also early in the morning. They usually met for lunch at one of the houses and then had dinner either at a restaurant or one of them would cook at home. Where ever they went, they had a great time. They also enjoyed going to movies when not watching them at one of their homes.

Then one day, the conversation turned to getting married. "Marilyn, remember when we talked about getting married before?" Michael asked.

"Yes, I sure do. I remember we had walked past a church where a wedding had been held. Remember the wedding party was out in front of the church getting pictures made," Marilyn answered.

"You said you wanted a small wedding. What are you thinking now? It's just my luck you'll want a huge destination wedding with a gigantic reception that will cost millions of dollars. Also, your wedding dress will have a twenty-foot-long train. You'll have fifteen bridesmaids….." Michael teased.

"How did you know! That's what I have always dreamed of! So sweet of you, Michael," Marilyn teased right back. "Nah, really, nothing has changed from when I was nineteen. I'd want a very simple wedding with only immediate family and a few friends. Simple gold bands---matching. Knee length wedding dress with lace sleeves---cream colored preferably. Pretty simple, huh?"

"Whew---thank goodness," he responded teasing her.

"After you and I work in our gardens tomorrow morning, why don't we go wedding band shopping?" Michael asked.

"Are you asking me to marry you, Michael?" Marilyn teased.

"No, not yet. I'm just saying we can go ring shopping---asking you comes next---when you least expect it," he answered slyly.

"Then aren't you getting the horse before the cart? What if I say 'no' and you're stuck with the ring?" she answered.

"Then I'll ask that cute waitress we like so much in the diner on eleventh street. In fact, now that I'm thinking about that, maybe I should ask her first and use you as a back-up. What do you think about that?"

Marilyn glared at him with her evil eye----"Ok, ok, just kidding!" Michael answered. "Nah, I've never been so sure of anything in my life. We were meant to be together from the time we met in college, and it is finally going to happen. I know I love you more than anything in this world, and I believe you love me the same way." *And I do*, she thought.

I can't believe this is really happening. I always dreamed of having a wedding with Michael, and now after all of this time, it is really going to happen.

4

The next day around noon, Michael and Marilyn grabbed a bite of lunch at the local diner and then went to Sterling's Jewelry Store. They found the perfect set of matching gold bands approximately a quarter of an inch wide. They decided to engrave the date August 13 on the inside---the date of their wedding. It was still some time away, so they'd have time to plan their simple wedding. Also, Michael would have time to formally ask her to marry him. It seemed backward in some ways, but it didn't really matter anymore---nothing else mattered anymore---as long as they were together.

Chapter Twenty-Six
Sharing Time Together

Michael and Marilyn enjoyed doing so many things together. Visiting the arboretum was a favorite, especially in the spring when the bulbs were just starting to bloom but also all summer long when they admired the large elephant ears and azaleas.

Arriving at the arboretum early in the morning, they caught a glimpse of the sunshine streaming through the tall canopies of the beautiful trees and could enjoy walking the paths before the park became busy with visitors. The plants were incredible! Marilyn enjoyed seeing the really large pots that greeted the visitors to the park and also the ones along the walkway, enticing people to see what artistic creation was next.

"Michael, we need to find a few really large pots like these so we can plant large elephant ears," Marilyn said with amazement when she saw the giant upright elephant ears reaching for the sky.

"Well, let's wait 'til we find the right house so we don't have to *move* them. OK? We'll find just the right house where you will have your tropical paradise and I can have a great vegetable garden. Someone has to keep food on the table, right?" he joked.

"Of course," Marilyn continued. "Once we get those pots set, no one is going to be able to move them! Do you think we'll be able to find what we need? I do need quite a bit of shade and I know you'll need quite a bit of sun for the vegetables."

"We will. Basically, any larger yard will work as long as it has taller, older trees. Maybe, we can find a place attached to an extra quarter acre or so. Who knows? We'll find it," he answered with confidence.

They continued walking down the paths to the various areas of the arboretum. Some spaces were filled with tropical plants spaced around small waterfalls and rock gardens. Others were in open sun and accentuated the bright colors of the full-sun flowers. Even the trees were interesting. Visitors could always see unusual trees of different shapes and colors. If Marilyn saw a seed pod, she was quick to borrow at least one seed to try on her own. She'd pop it into her pocket for future use.

Michael liked the experimental garden section. The specialists experimented with different kinds of flowers and shrubs in hopes of finding the perfect species for the area. "Oh, Michael---look at these hydrangeas! I've never seen such huge flowers! We must try to find these to grow ourselves!" Marilyn exclaimed with excitement. Michael knew he needed to make a note of those particular hydrangeas for their future garden.

This year when they approached the front gate of the park, Marilyn noticed some huge pots at the entrance, but they were filled with black elephant eats! They were beautiful. She had never seen black ones before. She had found bulbs at the local nursery that were called black elephant ears but in reality, they just had a stem that was a darker gray color. The leave itself was as green as the others. So, to see a plant with leaves so dark that they looked black was truly a sight to see. She was mesmerized. Asking the attendant about them, she found out that they came to the United States quite recently from Hawaii. They need a lot of water and prefer almost full sun. Without the sun, they will not have the dark black leaves that make them so pretty. Marilyn made another mental note about these beautiful plants.

They reached a part of the park that had several small fountains. It was so peaceful, hearing the trickling of the water in the fountain. "Michael, do you think we could add a water feature at our new house so we could hear the water while we sit out in our garden? I've always wanted a fountain," Marilyn mentioned.

"Of course, we can. We can do anything we want. If you want a fountain---a fountain it is. Ya just need to tell me what to look for or how to build it. I can get a friend of mine who's in the business to build one for us. Be thinking how ya want it," Michael answered.

Holding around each other's waists, they continued down the path toward the gazebo. The most

175

beautiful blue flowers lined the walkway, accented by bright yellow flowers behind them. Marilyn didn't know if she could keep all the notes in her head that she was accumulating during their walk. Everything was just so pretty. *Life is really good,* she thought. *If I had no flowers…if I had no plants…..if I had no yard…..it wouldn't matter. As long as I have Michael, nothing else in the world matters anymore. But having Michael and all the things I love is absolutely perfect!* She knew Michael felt the same way she did.

2

In the evenings, as Marilyn read or worked on crocheting her afghans, Michael watched the news or some movie on television. They loved being together after dinner and would rather have dinner at home than in any restaurant.

"It's not that I don't appreciate good restaurant food," Marilyn explained, "But, I just don't want to waste time driving there, or standing in line waiting for a table, or getting out when it's really cold and dark outside. I just love the coziness of our home and the quality of life we have here. Driving in a car is no kind of quality of life. Now, I do admit that we enjoy talking to and from and during, but wouldn't you rather be at home? I like the quietness----the privacy----am I spoiled?"

"You're not spoiled. You just know what you like. I just worry that you feel you have to cook after a long day of tutoring or gardening," Michael added. "Are ya sure ya don't mind?"

"I'll be the first one to tell ya if I do," Marilyn answered. "It's so easy to just whip out a meal and then we have more time here together. I also don't usually overeat that way, either. If we eat out, I have no self-discipline. I'll eat the entire plate!"

They both seemed to really like staying at home as much as possible.

3

Since finding Dean, everyone on both sides tried to get together as often as possible. Dean's parents, and Michael's parents became close friends after finding out that they adopted twins separately many years ago. At first when they found out, they were just shocked. Then the shock turned into anger when they realized that the boys should have been able to spend their childhood and young adulthood together. They hired an attorney who looked into the adoption agency at the university hospital and found out that Dean and Michael were part of an experiment about identical twins growing up apart. The families knew that over the years, doctors tested the boys and had their parents fill out long questionnaires, but they didn't know it involved identical twins. They were told it was just a study about adopted children and they were happy to accommodate.

The families found out that the adoption agency had closed down many years ago and the studies concerning twins was sealed and archived at the university. Under court order, they were able to get the information they requested, but it really didn't provide them any clues on why the study would keep the parents in the dark about the other twin other than the fact that parents would not have allowed the study to continue. No one would have permitted twins to be separated at birth. Michael and Dean didn't have time to worry about what happened when they were adopted. They had too many things to catch up on. They wanted to spend as much time together as they could----they were brothers after all.

On one of the family gatherings, everyone sat around and discussed other likenesses between the two boys. The discussion focused on medical information. "Dean had his tonsils out when he was pretty young. Remember, he would always have sore throats and ear infections until his tonsils were finally removed?" Dean's father said looking toward Deans mother.

"Yes, I remember he was just ten years old because that was the same year Aunt Julie passed away. Remember, we were at the hospital with Dean when we got the news. I'll never forget it," she answered.

"Michael was ten, too!" Michael's mother exclaimed. "He was just beginning fourth grade and he didn't want to miss school until we told him he could have all of the ice cream he wanted. Then he was all for it!" The group laughed pointing at Michael.

"Then, I guess the next thing was the bout with pneumonia. That was a little scary," Mr. Moran added. "When do you think that was?" he asked turning toward his wife.

"Don't you remember? He was just thirteen. He had just had a terrible flu that settled in his chest. It got so bad that he had trouble breathing so we rushed him to the emergency room. Sure enough, he had developed a case of pneumonia," she answered.

Dean's parents looked at each other in amazement. "Dean had pneumonia and it happened in about the same way. He was also thirteen. How can this be?" his father answered with a puzzled look on his face.

"OK, I have one for ya. Did Michael ever have a black eye?" Dean's father asked remember the time that Dean caught a ball and it flipped up and hit him right in the eye, causing a big black eye. Dean didn't mind because he thought it would be cool to go to school with a black eye. He was fifteen.

"You have us there. Nah, I don't remember Michael ever having a black eye," Michael's dad answered before Michael interrupted him.

"Yes, I did! Don't ya remember? We were playing catch out the backyard and I leaned down to catch a grounder when it hit a rock and jumped right up hitting me in the right eye. I had a shiner for a whole week or more. Don't ya remember?" he asked.

"Oh, yeah, I guess I do remember once ya mention it. You were pretty cute. So how old were you about?" his father asked.

"I was fifteen. I had just finished my ninth-grade year and it was at the beginning of summer," Michael responded. Everyone looked around at each other with amazement.

Dean jumped in, "People would ask me what happened all that week. I told them, 'You should have seen the other guy!'" The group laughed.

It was uncanny how the boys' lives parallel each other. Not just that they had some of the same ailments growing up, but that they had them at exactly the same age!

Chapter Twenty-Seven
A Fun-Loving Trio

Michael and Marilyn enjoyed Dean's company immensely. They always laughed whenever they were together and, sometimes, Marilyn didn't know who was on the phone, since the two sounded so much alike. Sometimes they tried to trick her, but she was usually smarter than they were.

Frequently, Dean would help Michael with the garden. Both men loved working in the yard, but mainly, both men loved eating the fruits of their hard work. They could cook like gourmet cooks so having fresh vegetables was perfect for them. Marilyn enjoyed them both very much. She'd often look at the two men and think how lucky she was to not only have found Michael again, but to have found someone who enhanced both of their lives. Dean was a very special person. Marilyn wanted the two men to be together as much as possible.

One of their favorite activities was watching movies together at Marilyn's house. The three of them would get together, make a really good dinner, and then settle in to watch a classic movie. They were all classic movie addicts. Michael and Dean always noticed the same things in the movie so their comments were always the same. Marilyn added another dimension to the commentary. The guys thought she was so intelligent---and she was.

"Hey, Michael, how is it that you were able to trick Marilyn into liking you?" Dean asked jokingly. Obviously, if she had met me first, you'd be out of the picture."

"You're dreaming, bro," Michael answered. "She knows a highly intelligent man when she sees one." The trio laughed uncontrollably.

2

One of the activities that the trio enjoyed very much was the state fair. It only came around once a year so the trio planned in advance and marked off that date on their calendars.

Since the state fair was in another city, they arranged to drive down on one day, rent a couple of hotel rooms for two nights, then drive back home. They always enjoyed the drive down. It was a time that conversation and jokes ruled the drive. Stopping on the drive to grab a bite to eat always ended in jokes and laughter, usually with the waitresses and other people in the restaurant. The men never met a stranger---ever. Marilyn just watched in amazement. When they gave the waitress a hard time, Marilyn told her, "Next time we're gonna come here, I'll call you ahead of time so you can call in sick that day."

After staying up late talking, the trio put on their comfortable clothes and walking shoes for a full day at the state fair. They usually went to the animal barns first. On this particular day, they were lucky enough to be there when the miniature horse shows were going on. Marilyn could barely contain herself. The tiny horses were perfectly groomed; their long manes were even curled to be shiny and wavy. "Look at their hooves!" cried Marilyn. "Their hooves are perfectly manicured----or would you say pedicured? Well, anyway, look how polished."

Every once in a while, a colt would let out a baby 'neigh' that was so cute. Marilyn was infatuated with them all.

"Hey, Michael----looks like Marilyn has fallen in love with something other than you. She doesn't look at you that way," Dean said laughing and punching Michael in his side softly.

"Yeah, I knew this was going to happen someday. I just didn't know it was going to be with a horse," he answered sadly. "Let's get her out of here before she decides to buy one of these things.

The trio walked down the hall of the barn and looked in every stall. Each stall was filled with fresh hay and the name of the horse and its owner were proudly displayed on every gate. "Precious Pal," My Baby," "Cutie Pie," Marilyn read each name as they passed by.

"Oh, I thought you were talking about me!" Michael said. "How disappointing!" Laughter rang out again.

The fair just wouldn't be the fair with all the food. After vising the animal barns, it was late morning and plenty late enough to start sampling all the junk food. They started with a corny dog and topped it off with a tall glass of lemonade. Then came the funnel cake, the caramel apples, and snow cones.

"Hey---go easy on that stuff," Michael called out as Marilyn purchased another caramel apple.

"It's an apple, for Pete's sake! Apples are healthy!" Marilyn yelled back.

"Whose Pete?" Dean answered trying to be funny. He didn't care what they said---he was having another corny dog. Then he walked by the foot-long hotdog stand and bought one of those.

"I thought you just ate a funnel cake!" Michael exclaimed. "And now a hot dog---not to mention the corny dog before that?"

"So---who are you----the food police? There are no guidelines restricting the order in which one should consume one's food items," Dean answered formally. "Therefore, I shall consume whatever food items I want to consume when I want to consume them."

Marilyn didn't mind one bit. She was basically on Dean's side, too, since she had a corn-on-the-cob after her caramel apple. "Yummm," she over-emphasized.

3

The midway was sparkling with lights of all colors. There was excitement in the air. Screams were coming from the various rides as the riders were turned upside down and sideways while circling around and around!

He guys looked at Marilyn in anticipation. 'Nope---nope---I don't do those," Marilyn said when the guys tried to get her to climb on one of the crazy rides.

"Ah, come on---be a sport," Dean said pushing Michael to say the same. "Look, we can wedge you in between the two of us, and you'll have a great time. It only turns upside down a few times."

Michael did egg Marilyn on until she acquiesced. "I don't like this one bit, but if you want me to do this, I will. Just make sure you both protect me and make sure I don't fall out when this thing turns upside down.

The trio was seated in the ride and the safety bar was pulled down over their laps. Before the ride even started, Marilyn started screaming. "What are you doing!!" Michael demanded. "The ride hasn't even started yet---get a grip!"

"I'd rather scream now so I'll be prepared when it *really* gets scary!" she answered covering up her eyes.

The ride began and Dean acted like he was trying to tell something to Michael without Marilyn hearing it. "Hey, on the count of three, throw Marilyn out of the car! She won't have far to fall!" Marilyn instantly tried to strangle Dean with her two hands.

They had a great time on the ride but Marilyn screamed the entire time. Even when their car got back to the ground, she was still screaming. "Remind me to refrain from asking Marilyn on another ride, Dean," said Michael. "I'd like to keep my ear drums intact for my old age."

The next thing on their agenda at the fair was the hoops shooting booth. The guys thought they could make the basketball hoop not realizing that the hoop was smaller and slightly thicker than a normal basketball hoop. Not a single shot went through the hoop. "Oh, man, I thought we still had some athletic ability left over from our high school days," Dean mentioned sadly. "What happened?"

"Could it be that y'all are about forty pounds heavier, about 40 years older, and your eyesight is failing?" Marilyn mentioned sarcastically.

"Boy, ya really know how to hit a guy when he's down. I thought you were a nice, sweet girl," Michael said.

"Can you trade her in for a nicer upgrade?" Dean asked kiddingly as he winked at Marilyn. He was crazy about her and she knew it. They were great friends.

The dart throwing at balloons didn't go much better. Nor did the rings over the goldfish bowls. "Who wants a stinky old fish, anyway!" Dean responded. "I wish we could at least win at *something* though!"

Marilyn tried her hand at dart throwing. On the very first try, she hit one of the largest balloons. Because of that, she was given the medium sized teddy bear of her choice. "This is a conspiracy," Michael said. "She paid off the attendant, no doubt."

"You are both so jealous. My highly refined dart-throwing skills have just been waiting to be realized. I should have given y'all lessons before you wasted your money," Marilyn answered sarcastically.

"Ok, highly refined dart-throwing person, let's see ya do it again. This will *really* tell us if you have a skill or if it is just a fluke----just coincidental," Dean popped off.

So, Marilyn stepped up to the plate---waved her hand around with the dart between her fingers---and threw it at the board. *Oh my gosh*, Marilyn thought to herself. *I've never even tried to throw darts. The first one was coincidental but I can't show that I don't know how!* She played the part very well. At the amazement of all watching, Marilyn's dart flew up at an unusual angle, much too high to hit a balloon, but then if came straight down hitting three balloons in a row as it made its way down. It was a totally freakish thing. That couldn't be done if someone practiced it every day for a year.

"Are ya kidding me?" Michael screamed. People all around the trio were whooping and hollering!

"I'm not believing this!" Dean added with amazement. Of course, Marilyn was totally blown away also. What started off as a weird throw turned out to burst three balloons in a row. She acted as though she meant to do what she did.

"What?" she asked. "What's the problem? I told you I had highly defined dart-throwing skills and this is just proof of that. It's easy."

"M'am?" the game attendant said shaking his head. "I've been doin' this for 'bout forty years now and I've never seen anything like this. Never---not once. Here---I'm givin' ya the biggest stuffed animal here. Gladly."

Marilyn could barely hold the baby-blue teddy bear with the red ribbon around its neck. It was almost as tall as Marilyn. As soon as the trio got into the crowd, they gave the teddy bear to a small child whose father agreed to carry it around until they could get it to their car. "So, you won this?" the father asked Michael as he took the bear from him.

"No, *I* didn't. *She* did," he said pointing to Marilyn who was smiling from ear to ear. "She has highly refined dart-throwing skills." *Things aren't always as they seem,* he thought.

The trio felt that they had had enough for the day. They had a great time eating, laughing, riding rides, playing games, looking at the animals, and enjoying the sights and sounds of the midway. But everyone was tired. They found their car, made their way back to their hotel, and enjoyed hot showers before crashing for the night.

Chapter Twenty-Eight
The Bucket List

On the drive back home, the threesome talked about everything that came to mind. "Do you guys have a bucket list?" Marilyn asked.

"A bucket list?" Dean asked sincerely. "What exactly is that?"

"It's a list of things that you want to do in your lifetime. Have you ever wanted to stand on a glacier in Alaska? Or, have you ever wanted to ride a bicycle across the state? Those are the type of things most people think about, but it can also be as varied as reading five classical books or riding a rollercoaster in several countries. Actually, I have a friend named Yvonne who has ridden a rollercoaster in every country in the world! That's quite a feat," Marilyn explained.

"OK, let's develop a bucket list for the three of us together. After all, won't we always be together, anyway?" Michael suggested.

"Great idea! Everyone can suggest activities and we can discuss them. Then we'll vote. We just can't do anything that one of us would abhor or be afraid to do. Let's pick activities that are good for all of us---for the three musketeers."

On the drive back home, they kept coming up with suggestions. "Skydiving," suggested Michael. He didn't know if he really wanted to do it or if he just wanted to hear the response he'd get from the others.

"Heck, NO!" Marilyn and Dean screamed simultaneously. "No way!"

"Ok, scratch that one off the list," Michael responded probably relieved.

"What about go-cart racing?" Dean suggested. "They aren't dangerous. You just drive around on a little track, but I bet it's fun. Why don't we add that to our list?"

"That's works for me," Marilyn answered. "Me, too!" Michael answered. "We have our first item on our bucket list!"

"Hey---I have something that I've really wanted to do for quite some time," Dean said. "I'd like to go on a real camping trip. I went on a camping trip when I was in Boy Scouts as a kid, but I wouldn't say it was a true camp out. We were in an enclosed area---totally safe---I understand that. But what about camping out in the wild? Anybody interested?"

"You mean with bears and coyotes and mountain lions and maybe an occasional dinosaur?" Marilyn asked.

"Ha ha. That is really funny. But, yes---there may be all kinds of wildlife out there," Dean answered. "Wouldn't it be fun?"

Michael looked at him with a puzzled look on his face. "I get the idea of camping out under the stars all wrapped up in a sleeping bag and nestled in our tents, but you have to deal with going to the bathroom in the woods and making a fire to cook your own food. Not to mention if a bear decides he wants your food more than you do."

"Or, if the bear wants *you* for his food!" Marilyn added. "That would be my luck!"

"How about if we rent a log cabin---which is almost like camping out---and we put up a tent outside just for you so that you can have your 'camping out' experience? You can go to the bathroom out in the woods and everything. Take a roll of toilet paper--- but you can't just throw it down so you have to---- well, ya get the picture. Michael said laughing.

"I agree with Michael," Marilyn added. "We'll even sit with you out in your tent until its actually time to go to bed. It'll be kind of like a slumber party! I had a million of those growing up. Just scream if a bear starts ripping up your tent---or a snake slithers into your sleeping bag. We'll come to your rescue if we actually hear you. Plus, at the end of our day of hiking and fishing when we are all hot and sweaty, Michael, and I will take a hot shower in the cabin but with your *real* camping experience, you'll get to wash off in the cold, icy river or just go without. Doesn't that sound like a lot of fun?"

"Ok, ok, ok," Dean responded. "Let's just do a log cabin experience with hikes and maybe some fishing. Hey—we could do canoeing also."

"Agreed!" the others chimed in.

Now the trio had two items on their bucket list: go-cart racing and a log cabin vacation in the woods with fishing, canoeing, and hiking.

It was time to stop for lunch so the threesome looked out for just the right place. They decided on getting a hamburger at Joe's Burger House in a small town on the way. They never turned down hamburgers.

While waiting for their food, they continued the conversation about their bucket list.

"Have you guys ever wanted to go to London?" Marilyn asked.

"I never thought of it much. Seems like things are mostly pretty old over there. Have you?" Dean answered.

"*That's* the point. Everything *is* old. The architecture is unbelievable, the castles and cathedrals are hard to believe, and the quaint towns outside of London still have thatched roofs!" Marilyn answered.

"Wow, thatched roofs. I don't know how I've managed to live my life without seeing those thatched roofs." Michael responded.

"Hey—let's get a little educated, guys. It'll do us all some good. You'll love what you see. And don't forget---there's Stonehenge," Marilyn said trying to convince the guys they needed to add London to their bucket list.

"Oh yeah---I've always wanted to see a bunch of ancient stones standing around in a circle. Fascinating!" Michael said just kidding Marilyn. He had always wanted to see Stonehenge but had just forgotten about it. Now he had a reason to go--- Marilyn wanted to go! He would do anything for her.

"What do ya think, Dean?" Marilyn asked.

"Count me in! Looks like we have three items on our bucket list, he answered.

The waitress delivered their food to the table and then asked them if they needed anything else. "We only need a few more items for our bucket list," Dean responded.

The little girl just stared at him, not understanding what he meant. When she went back to the kitchen, she asked her fellow workers, "Have you ever heard of writing a list on a bucket?"

Chapter Twenty-Nine
Identical Isn't Identical Anymore

As the twins grew older, they looked different.
Over the years, the *identical* part didn't hold up, but
they still looked very much alike. Their eyes were
the same and they were the same height. Their
hands were one of their distinguishing features.
Both men had large hands with short fingers. Dean
gained a little more weight than Michael had and he
had more of a mid-section----Michael called it a
beer belly. Dean's hair was a little thinner on top.
Michael's face looked thinner. It was easy to tell
the guys apart. There were no 'twin capers' like the
ones they played on people when they were young
and looked exactly alike. They continued to
reminisce about those hilarious days.

Michael noticed that when they were out working
in his garden, Dean had to sometimes sit down and
take a little rest. He always blamed it on the heat.
Sometimes when Michael and Dean were moving
pots in the yard, Dean appeared more out of breath.
He sweated more profusely and stopped to take
breaks frequently. At first Michael didn't notice but
then he realized Dean's difficulty wasn't normal. It
was Michael who convinced Dean to get checked
out.

Dean made an appointment and saw a cardiologist
who was also Michael's friend. Dean probably got
in earlier because Michael had that connection. In
the back of Michael's mind, he wondered if he

would start feeling the same symptoms---after all they were alike in most every way. He rationalized Dean's symptoms by saying that Dean had gained a lot of weight, and it was the weight that caused him to be short of breath. There was some denial going on.

The cardiologist put Dean through several tests. In addition to high blood pressure, Dean unexpectedly had a blockage that could be life threatening. He didn't even know it at the time, but then recalled that he had been having some shortness of breath after just a short walk or a little dizziness when standing up. In addition, he had pain in his shoulder and back. His angiogram showed a considerable blockage in one of his main arteries with partial blockage in the others. Even though Dean ate well and avoided the usual high fats and cholesterol foods, he still had calcium build up that resulted in the blockage.

The doctor put him on one medication for blood pressure and one for cholesterol. In addition, he was prescribed medication for heart failure. Dean actually started feeling much better. Michael and Marilyn were relieved. He seemed to be on the mend. The doctor monitored his condition closely to make sure his condition was improving. When Dean's blockage wasn't improving with medication, the doctor announced that he would need angioplasty and a stent. At least it wasn't going to be bypass surgery which would have been much more dangerous.

Dean talked to Michael about his condition. "Michael, I'm a little concerned about what's goin' on with me. I don't feel that bad, other than being short of breath, but I feel it may be worse than I think," Dean said acting quite seriously.

"Oh, come on, Dean. Ya know you're gonna be just fine. The docs will open up that blockage, put a stent in there to keep it open, and you'll be as good as new in no time---really. I have no doubt," Michael replied in every attempt to make Dean feel better about the procedure.

"You're probably right. I just have a funny feeling about it," he answered. "Then again, if it's my time, it's my time. Haven't we had a blast these last thirty years? You're the greatest brother anyone could ever have. I love ya, bro," he said sincerely.

"Don't even think about it. You'll see. And yep---best thirty years of my life. I love you, too," Michael responded.

Chapter Thirty
An Unexpected Blow

Marilyn was concerned about Michael since the two men were identical twins and seemed to share most ailments and health issues during their lifetime. She prodded Michael into getting checked out to prevent any difficulties in the future.

Dean went to the doctor for all the necessary tests that he needed for the angioplasty procedure to open the blockage. It was to be a simple, yet serious, procedure. Marilyn and Michael didn't think there was anything to worry about. But then, something happened. Even though the procedure was going well, Dean took a turn on the operating table and his heart stopped. There was no good explanation for that happening. The medical team did everything they could to resuscitate him; his heart would not respond to their attempts. The doctors had to surmise that it was just Dean's time. They had no medical reason why Dean's heart just stopped. It just did.

Marilyn and Michael were devastated at their loss. They had enjoyed his company almost every day. Laughter filled their home when they were together. They thought they had many more years to spend together and could grow old together. Then Marilyn became very worried. *What if this happens to Michael? It can't. He's so healthy, but we thought Dean was healthy, too. Oh, God, don't let this happen to Michael. I need him with me.*

One day when Marilyn was reading, she remembered a short story that she taught her high school students when she taught English. It was titled, "Flowers for Algernon." Algernon was a little mouse that lived in a science lab. He became part of an experiment that included a 32-year-old mentally challenged young man, Charlie Gordon.

Charlie became an experiment at the Beekman College Center for Retarded Adults. He worked with Dr. Strauss and Miss Kinnian in an experiment that had only been tried on animals previously. Charlie took all kinds of psychological and intelligence tests. Then one day, Dr. Strauss took Charlie to the lab where the animals were kept. He took out a tiny white mouse and place it in a maze to show Charlie how the mouse could run through the maze. Charlie was unable to find his way through the maze using an electric wand to maneuver through the pathways. He thought Algernon was the smartest mouse he had ever seen.

The experiment involved an operation on Charlie's brain. The same operation had been done on Algernon. If the operation were successful, Charlie would become very smart and would be able to do many things that he would otherwise never be able to do. After the surgery, he slowly started getting smarter, but it was a slow process. Every day, he visited the lab to watch how Algernon performed his tasks. Eventually, Charlie became so smart that he was able to speak several languages, to write very intelligent books, and work very difficult mathematical equations. He became a genius. But then something happened. He noticed that Algernon was starting to lose his ability to go through the mazes quickly. Other tests that Algernon performed perfectly before were not being done satisfactorily. Charlie realized that if Algernon was losing his intelligence, that he, too, would lose his. After all, Charlie had the same operation that Algernon had had. Slowly, Charlie started losing his ability to read, to speak languages, or to do math problems. He ended up in the same job he had had before, and he didn't really know the difference. He checked himself into another home for mentally challenged adults.

Marilyn remembered the story and was afraid that Michael could feel the same way about Dean. If Dean died of a heart attack, would Michael see the handwriting on the wall? Would he think that he would die of a heart attack also? It seemed that other sicknesses and illnesses happened to both of them at approximately the same time. This was a scary thought. She didn't mention the story to Michael and she didn't mention her fear, either.

3

Several months went by and August was approaching. Michael and Marilyn made more plans for their wedding. It was sad that Dean was going to be the best man and now he would not be there. Marilyn's sister, Brenda, would be her maid of honor and one of Michael's friends, Bill, would be the best man. Marilyn found just the right dress----a cream-colored knee length dress with long, lace sleeves. It was exactly what she was looking for.

Since Michael had not officially proposed, he thought about options to make it the best proposal ever. Finally, he decided on something pretty simple. After all, Marilyn always wanted everything to be very simple. Michael took her to a romantic restaurant where they had a wonderful, delicious and very private dinner, and then he had the waiter hand Marilyn the dessert menu. Opening the menu, Marilyn saw a note that said, *Marilyn, Will You Marry Me?* Michael, knelt down on one knee next to Marilyn. She smiled at him and couldn't keep the tears from streaming down her face. "Will you marry me, Marilyn?" Michael asked as he held her hand.

"Of course, I will!" she answered as she hugged him, not letting go. "I love you so much."

They stood and held each other for several minutes. Neither wanted to let go. It was the best feeling in the world. *Life is so good*, they both thought.

Chapter Thirty-One
Michael's Premonition

The proposal went beautifully---better than Michael had even hoped for. It was simple; it was private; it was just what Marilyn wanted. Even though both of them were still very saddened by Dean's death, they never talked about what made them sad. Instead, they talked about all of the really good times they had with Dean and how blessed they were to have found him. Making him a part of their lives was a real blessing for all of them---including Dean.

Michael could never get away from the idea that kept popping into his head when he thought of Dean. He couldn't just leave things to chance. He had to take steps to ensure that if anything happened to him, Marilyn would be taken care of for the rest of her life. He met with his financial advisor and estate attorney to put all of his things in order. He had no children from any previous marriage, and he had already taken care of setting up trust funds for his nieces and nephews and other family members. He wanted to take care of Marilyn's parents and then provide a wonderful retirement for Marilyn to enjoy and to share with anyone she wanted.

The last thing he did was to write a letter that would be hand delivered to Marilyn in the case of his death. If he were to die before their wedding in August, he had one letter prepared. If he were to die after their wedding, he had another letter prepared. Either way, Marilyn would be totally cared for and Michael's letter to her would explain how much he loved her. That all he wanted to do. Then he prayed that God would grant him the time-- many years---to spend with Marilyn.

"Michael," his attorney Arthur said, "I'm very happy to do this for you, but I know you are going to live to be a crotchety old man that I'm going to have to put up with for many years to come."

"I hope you're right, my man," Michael responded laughing. "I hope I get to be that crotchety old man! But just in case, you know what to do. Do we need to rehearse it?"

"I think I've got it," Arthur answered.

Chapter Thirty-Two
Marilyn's Angel Garden

Marilyn had always loved angels. She had angel statues in the house and many large ones out in her garden area. In the area she called her Secret Angel Garden, she had a kneeling angel statue saying a prayer over the markers of several friends and family members who had passed. She added a marker for Dean and put it in the very front. It saddened her greatly, but it was also soothing to know that he was in a beautiful place and that someday they would see him again. After a long day gardening, it was peaceful to sit and look at the markers and remember the people whom she loved.

As she looked at her maternal grandmother's marker, she remembered riding her bicycle a few blocks to where her grandmother lived. She took her coloring books and crayons and would color pictures while lying on the living room floor. Most of the time, her grandfather was sitting in his comfortable chair asleep in the same room. He slept most of the time while in his chair. Then, Marilyn would climb on her bike and drive back home. Her grandfather died of a heart attack in his garden. He had a history of heart difficulties. He also had a history of kidney stones. Marilyn was very young when he passed. She also remembered seeing the quilting frame that her grandmother used to make homemade quilts. The fabric was stretched around the frame and held there with clamps. Friends would sit around the frame and stitch quilting into the quilt. Marilyn has never seen that since.

When she saw her father's marker, she remembered so many things from her childhood. Her father could make and fix just about everything. He taught her that she could do anything also. So, Marilyn grew up believing she could do anything she wanted to do. Once when just a young girl, she wanted to fix a broken electric razor. Being extra careful not to touch anything inside while the razor was plugged in, she carefully unplugged the razor and then unscrewed the case to reveal the motor. She located the lose wire and fixed it. She plugged the razor back in to the electrical socket. Very carefully, she touched a part of the mechanism, but it must have been a live part. A shot of electricity climbed right up her arm. It was scary! She decided to leave the electrical work to her dad.

She remembered the day her father told her and her sister that they were going to the farm store to buy some baby chicks. She was excited! She loved little animals and her sister did, too. What she didn't know was that buying the baby chicks wasn't so they would have little pets. It was because her father wanted to teach her how to run a business. Run a business! What did that mean? Well, she soon found out.

Picking up the baby chicks was quite exciting. There were two boxes with fifty chicks in each box. They were yellow and only about two inches tall---

so cute. The boxes had wholes all along the sides about the size of quarters. Marilyn and her sister could see the little yellow chicks peeking their heads through the holes. When they arrived home, the baby chicks were taken out of the boxes and were placed in a cage on the top of a table with warming lights on each end. The chicks would be kept warm by the lights. As they grew, they were placed in a larger pen. Finally, they were old enough to be called 'fryers' by Marilyn's father. What did that mean? Unfortunately, Marilyn and her sister soon found out. Their father sold the 'fryers' to the neighbors but first he chopped off their heads and cleaned them for his customers. Marilyn remembers the hatchet that her father used to chop off their heads. The most gruesome thing Marilyn remembered was how the chickens continued to run and flop around even after they lost their heads! She thought they were still alive!

That same hatchet played another important role in Marilyn's memory. After adopting a cute little, fluffy puppy, her father felt he would be much cuter if he did not have a tail. Really? He sharpened his hatchet on a sharpening wheel and then poured alcohol over the tail of the puppy where the cut was going to be. He placed the puppy's tail on a wooden block then "whack!" The tail fell to the ground. The puppy let out a slight "Yip" and that was all there was to that. At least Dad didn't chop his head off!!!

When Marilyn saw her paternal grandmother's marker in the Angel Garden, she remembered being in her grandmother's house every day. Her grandmother lived next door. She was Norwegian and taught Marilyn to count to ten in that language at an early age. She always thought Marilyn was too skinny so every time Marilyn saw her, her grandmother tried to get her to eat Fig Newton cookies. Marilyn hated those cookies. Even today Marilyn doesn't like them. She remembered her grandmother living in a very small house. She collected sheets that she got saving green stamps from buying groceries. She didn't need all of those sheets but that is what she got every time. Marilyn couldn't remember how old she was when she passed away but the marker helped Marilyn remember her.

Marilyn didn't have as many memories concerning her paternal grandfather. She remembered he was very thin and tall. After her grandmother died, he came to live with Marilyn and her family. He spent his day watching television and just sitting. Marilyn doesn't remember having any conversations with him. It was a short period of time, before he went to the hospital and died there. The only thing Marilyn remembered about his death is that he looked up, called out, "Papa," and then closed his eyes and died. Marilyn's father told her that story. He was there to witness it.

Marilyn had markers not only for family members but also for friends who passed. One was for Elaine who was the colleague who hired Marilyn at one of her school districts. One was for Bo who was a good friend and colleague who died too soon, also. Then two of the nicest men who worked for the district were tragically taken when only 50 and 55 years of age from cancer. Marilyn thought of them as she sat staring at their markers—Jon and Kris. Marilyn's markers were her way of honoring their lives and keeping them in her memory.

Unfortunately, and sadly, the number of markers increased over the years.

Chapter Thirty-Three
Another Unexpected Tragedy

Michael loved working in his vegetable garden. Both Michael and Marilyn enjoyed picking the fruits of his labor and cooking them for dinner. In no time at all, he had tall stalks of bright green okra, ruby red tomatoes clinging to their vines, large cucumbers trailing along the ground, and tall stalks of white and yellow corn. There is nothing that tastes as good as fresh vegetables grown in totally organic soil. Michael was a master at it. He was quite proud of his garden and loved showing it off to the neighbors.

One morning while talking to his neighbor about politics, Michael caught a glimpse of a skunk running into the garden. He knew the skunk could be very detrimental to his vegetables. Excitedly, he took a jogging step or two but then fell to the ground. The neighbor ran into the house to call the ambulance. They rushed him to the hospital where he was pronounced dead. He had had a major heart attack and was probably dead before he reached the ground, according to the doctors who examined him. Marilyn was told in the private waiting room at the hospital. *No---not again---I can't lose Michael again. He is my life. I need him,* she cried after hearing the bad news.

After all the friends and family left her house that evening, she lay in bed thinking about her life. I never had the chance to marry Michael because of a freak coincidence. I never married anyone else because no one could really measure up to what I thought Michael was. Now, in my later years, I was going to have my first and only wedding---the only wedding in my entire life, and it has been taken from me. The love of my life has been taken from me once again. What do I have to live for? Marilyn cried herself to sleep as she would do for many, many nights to come.

2

Michael's financial advisor/estate attorney, Arthur Salinas, made a special trip to see Marilyn a few days after Michael's death.

"Marilyn, after Dean's death, Michael was concerned about his own well-being, so he did a few things that he wanted me to tell you about in the case that something happened to him, also. First of all, I must tell you that Michael loved you more than anything else in this world. He was so happy that the two of you had gotten back together and he was ecstatic that you were going to be married. I've personally never seen him so happy in all the years I have known him."

Then he continued, "Marilyn, Michael was a very successful business man and investor. He has set up trust funds so that you and your parents will be set financially for the rest of your lives. In fact, better than just *set* financially. Your parents will have everything that they need, and you will have an access of three-quarters of a million dollars at your disposal every year until you die. You can do whatever you want with it—take your parents on cruises, take your sister to Europe….anything you want."

Smiling, he added, "He also set aside a half of a million dollars for the home that the two of you were going to share together. He really wants you to pick out a house you'll be comfortable living in. He also mentioned finding a house with a beautiful garden area in the back. Basically, he didn't want you to *want* for anything." Marilyn was shocked. She knew that Michael had been very successful in his businesses, but she never knew he was quite *that* successful.

"Finally," he added, pulling an envelope out of his coat pocket. "Michael wanted me to hand deliver this to you personally. He wants you to read it after I leave."

Marilyn slowly took the letter from Arthur's hand and stared at it for a few seconds. "He wanted you to give this to me? How did he know?"

"He really didn't know that he would die. When Dean passed away from the heart attack, Michael worried that he would meet the same fate as his brother. So many things in their lives paralleled, you know. He just wanted to be prepared in case something did happen to him, also. That's why he set up the trust funds, and why he wrote this letter.

Marilyn thanked Arthur for everything and helped him out the front door. Just as he walked out, he turned quickly and said, "Oh, I almost forgot---- here, this is also for you from Michael." Arthur reached in his other coat pocket and handed Marilyn a small package of M&M's. "He said you would understand." *Of course, of course----I understand. Michael, you beat me again,* Marilyn thought with a smile on her face.

Turning to the living room, Marilyn sat in her favorite chair and slowly opened the letter:

Dearest Marilyn,

If you are reading this letter personally handed to you from Arthur, it is only because I have died and I have very important things to say to you. I never ever wanted to leave you, but both you and I knew this could happen. I just couldn't take the chance after Dean passed to leave this world without telling you exactly how I feel about you. We should have been together from the very beginning, but it just wasn't meant to be. Thank goodness that later on, we figured out what happened, and we were both in the position to be together again. Finding your love again made me the happiest man in the world. All the money in the world can't make a person happy; it only comes about when a person finds true love. I found you---my true love. If love is a grain of sand, then the love I have for you is greater than the number of grains of sand on all the beaches of the world. If love is a star in the sky, then my love for you is greater than the number of stars in the universe. If love is a drop of water, then my love for you is greater than all the water in the oceans around the world. I don't know any other way to explain how much I love you. Our marriage on August 13 was going to be the very best day of my life. I wanted to marry you more than anything---- more than anything. I wanted to be your husband and to love and care for you forever. Now I know that will never be. Now, I want you to have a wonderful, long life. Be happy. Do everything you've always wanted to do. Then someday when you pass, I will return to take you home. I'll be there for you.

I Love You,
Michael

Marilyn held onto the letter just staring at it for a few minutes. Then she slowly folded it back up and slid it into the envelope. Tears streamed down her face. She loved Michael so much and wanted to marry him so much but now that would never be. His letter also mentioned how much he wanted to marry her. *When I get to heaven, I'm going to ask God why he took Michael from me right at this time. If he could have just waited a few more months. I'm sorry, God. I know not to question you. Forgive me. I'm just human.*

Marilyn appreciated all of the nice cards and letters of condolences she received in the days after Michael's death leading up to his funeral. His viewing was set for the day before the funeral----- August 13. *How ironic----this is the date Michael engraved in our wedding rings---the date of our wedding. Now, instead of a wedding, there is going to be his viewing. How can I make it through this?* Marilyn woke up after a sleepless night and prepared to do one of the hardest things she would ever have to do----say goodbye to Michael. She pulled out her black dress, the only one she owned and lay it on the bed. The dress she bought to get married in kept grabbing her attention. It was quite lovely---a cream-colored, knee-length dress with long lace sleeves. She had always wanted to be married in a dress with long, lace sleeves. Slowly, she hung the black dress back in the closet and took out the other dress. *I'm going to wear this one. No one will care that I'm not in black. I'll wear black tomorrow to the funeral. I want to wear this one today.*

Michael's viewing was to be held from 10:00am to 12:00pm in Englund's Funeral Home. Marilyn had met the owners and was very pleased with the kindness they showed during her time of sorrow.

Michael's casket was absolutely beautiful. It was a dark, very shiny mahogany with brass hardware. Inside, the tufted lining was an off-white satin that made his dark navy suit look exquisite. Marilyn picked out his favorite burgundy tie. His casket was placed in a beautiful room just past the receptionist desk down the hall. Friends and family members gathered to talk to Marilyn and then to view his body on the other side of the room. The funeral home had done an outstanding job preparing his body---mourners mentioned that he looked more alive than dead. Near the end of the viewing time, everyone had pretty much left and Marilyn was alone for the first time. Robert, the attendant to the viewing stood by the door to the room.

"Miss Marilyn?" he gently asked walking through the open door. "Do ya want to spend a little more time with him before you go?" He knew and Marilyn knew, that when she walked out of the room, she would never see Michael ever again.

"Yes, Robert, if you don't mind. Would it be OK if I run to the car to retrieve something and then spend a few more minutes here with Michael?" she asked quietly.

"Absolutely, Miss Marilyn. You do whatever you want. I'm here for you. You take your time," he answered.

With that, Marilyn walked down the hall, past the receptionist desk and out to her car. Once at the car, she picked up a small, velvet box and a larger box approximately the size of a hat box. She returned to the room and set the boxes down. Then she opened the large box and removed a beautiful pink and white rose bouquet with white and pink satin ribbons hanging down. She stood by Michael's casket, closed her eyes, and lowered her head. Thoughts of her wedding filled her heart. For a few minutes she could dream. She dreamed of walking down the aisle to join Michael at the altar. He would be smiling at her and she at him. She would look into his eyes with every step she took toward him. Then arriving next to him, he would take her hand and they would turn to the minister. For a few minutes, Marilyn and Michael were actually there at the altar together. Her dream was real.

Then, Marilyn removed the two, gold wedding bands from the velvet box. She placed one on her ring finger and then placed one on Michael's ring finger. Then she looked at Michael in his dark suit, and said, "With this ring… I thee wed." *I love you, Michael, with all my heart.*

Marilyn walked out of the room. Robert was standing beside the door to be near if she needed him. "Thank you, Robert. You have been so kind to me. Thanks for letting me spend this time with Michael." She hugged him gently.

Robert hugged her back and then watched as she turned and walked away. He felt sorry for her. He always felt sorry for the grieving who were left behind, but it was more than normal with Marilyn. He knew the history; he knew the story.

Marilyn walked down the hallway toward the receptionist desk. Leslie—the young girl at the desk saw Marilyn carrying the beautiful bouquet and said, "Miss Marilyn! I believe that is the prettiest bouquet I've ever seen."

"Yes, it *is* beautiful, isn't it?" Marilyn answered smiling sweetly.

Marilyn walked past the desk and out the front door. To the immediate right lay a beautiful, serene garden with a carved-wooden bench and multitudes of flowers of different colors and shapes. The fern and other lush, green plants made a wonderful backdrop to such a pleasant area. Marilyn looked at the garden, smiled, glanced down at the shiny gold wedding band on her left hand, turned around with her back to the garden, and threw her bouquet over her right shoulder. She imagined her college girlfriends jumping up to catch the bouquet as it flies through the air toward them; the pink and white ribbons trail the roses in an arch toward the wooden bench. The bouquet drops to the ground….. Marilyn smiled. She never looked back. Then she walked down the sidewalk to her car.

The End

55988692R00130

Made in the USA
Middletown, DE
20 July 2019